GRIMOIRE
Tracked by Terror

by Brad Strickland

DIAL BOOKS FOR
YOUNG READERS

DIAL BOOKS FOR YOUNG READERS
A division of Penguin Young Readers Group
Published by The Penguin Group
Penguin Group (USA) Inc., 375 Hudson Street, New York, NY 10014, U.S.A.
Penguin Group (Canada), 90 Eglinton Avenue East, Suite 700, Toronto, Ontario, Canada M4P 2Y3
(a division of Pearson Penguin Canada Inc.)
Penguin Books Ltd, 80 Strand, London WC2R 0RL, England
Penguin Ireland, 25 St. Stephen's Green, Dublin 2, Ireland (a division of Penguin Books Ltd)
Penguin Group (Australia), 250 Camberwell Road, Camberwell, Victoria 3124, Australia
(a division of Pearson Australia Group Pty Ltd)
Penguin Books India Pvt Ltd, 11 Community Centre, Panchsheel Park, New Delhi - 110 017, India
Penguin Group (NZ), Cnr Airborne and Rosedale Roads, Albany, Auckland 1310, New Zealand
(a division of Pearson New Zealand Ltd)
Penguin Books (South Africa) (Pty) Ltd, 24 Sturdee Avenue, Rosebank,
Johannesburg 2196, South Africa
Penguin Books Ltd, Registered Offices: 80 Strand, London WC2R 0RL, England

Designed by Jasmin Rubero
Text set in Centaur MT
Printed in the U.S.A.
1 3 5 7 9 10 8 6 4 2
Library of Congress Cataloging-in-Publication Data
Strickland, Brad.
Grimoire : tracked by terror / by Brad Strickland.
p.   cm.
Sequel to: Grimoire: the curse of the Midions.
Summary: Jarvey Midion becomes lost again
within the pages of the Grimoire, a powerful book of spells,
where he must navigate complex worlds and battle new and more evil Midions.
ISBN 978-0-8037-3061-8
[1. Space and time—Fiction. 2. Magic—Fiction. 3. Fantasy.] I. Title. II. Title: Tracked by terror.
PZ7.S9166Gt 2007
[Fic]—dc22
2007004154

To G.K.,
who liked my sonnet

Table of Contents

Dreams May Come

Jarvey Midion woke with a gasp and scrambled out of his bed, trying to escape the nightmare. He was twelve years old, and in all those twelve years he had never had a dream as horrible as that one. It had been about a bizarre old man named Siyamon Midion, who was some kind of evil sorcerer, and his book of dire magic spells, the Grimoire. It had been about his parents vanishing, and about Jarvey being hunted . . . it was fading away, the way dreams do.

Jarvey hated nightmares. When he was younger, sometimes he'd wake up at night screaming in terror, and his parents would come rushing in. Afterward, when he realized none of the nightmare had been real and that he had scared his mom and dad for nothing, Jarvey always felt deeply ashamed.

Well, he hadn't yelled out in a long time, and the bad dreams always faded away once he was fully awake. He looked over at the red digital readout of the clock radio: 5:03.

For a few minutes he lay on his side, letting his heart slow to its normal rate and watching the minutes change. By the time 5:21 appeared, Jarvey decided he wouldn't be able to fall asleep again. The dream had upset him too much, particularly the part where his parents—

Jarvey couldn't stand to complete the thought. Instead he slipped out of bed and felt around on the wall for the light switch. For just an instant he had the sick feeling that the light was going to show something terrible, but it only revealed his room. His desk stood cluttered with books and papers left over from school, which had just wound up for the summer. A little pile of game cartridges lay on the floor beside his bed, and he remembered that he had been playing Galactic Death Run on his GameMax machine before dozing off. Yesterday's jeans, socks, and shoes lay scattered on the floor.

Jarvey quietly and quickly got dressed, not bothering

with socks but pulling his sneakers onto his bare feet, and stepped out onto the darkened landing outside his room. His parents' bedroom door was closed, and from behind it came the sawing-wood sound of Jarvey's dad snoring. No evil sorcerer had spirited his mom and dad away. It was just a dream.

His knees feeling weak with relief, Jarvey went downstairs. The house lay silent. Still feeling oddly uneasy, Jarvey unlocked and opened the front door. A full moon sailed directly overhead, making the lawn a silvery, deep-shadowed sweep. Jarvey stepped outside. The familiar neighborhood spread out around him. For a second he wondered why he didn't hear any night sounds at all, and then as if in response, the cicadas and crickets struck up, a buzzing, chirping chorus. Taking a deep breath of cool morning air, even noticing the sweetish smell of recently mowed grass, Jarvey stood on the lawn beneath the moon, wondering why he had the persistent feeling that something was wrong.

Wait—shouldn't a full moon be about to set this close to dawn? But there it hung, straight overhead in a starless black sky. The silvery disk moved in a grotesque, slow dance in the sky, its outline shimmering as if waves of heated air were passing over it.

Then it glimmered into a gigantic face, an evil old

man's face with cruel, deep-set eyes and a leering, grin-
ning mouth that revealed crooked, stained teeth. "I see-ee
you," rasped a high-pitched, taunting voice.

Jarvey bolted toward the house, yelling in alarm when
he realized it had disappeared. So had the neighborhood,
even the lawn.

Jarvey screamed, "Mom! Dad!"

From overhead a contemptuous high-pitched cackle
laughed at him, and the sneering old voice mocked, "Mo-
om! Da-ad!" Jarvey staggered under the force of the man's
grating laughter, louder than a hurricane, louder than the
end of the world—

"Jarvey! Wake up!"

Jarvey flinched away from the hand shaking his shoulder, rolled, scrambled up onto all fours, and crouched
there, his eyes wide and staring.

Betsy Dare drew her hand back as if she had burned
herself. "What's wrong with you?"

For a moment Jarvey couldn't say anything. His heart
thudded in his throat, choking off the words. "Dream,"
he croaked at last, gasping for air.

But whether he meant his home had been the dream, or
the transformed moon, or even being awakened by Betsy,
he could not at that moment tell.

✳ ✳ ✳

Some time later, Betsy asked, "Are you ready to try to get into another chapter?"

It was an odd thing to say, but in fact the two of them were lost in the pages of a book, and not in the way an eager reader gets lost. Jarvey had been thrown into the book by the evil Siyamon Midion, who, along with Jarvey's dad, had been one of the people named in a mysterious will. To claim his inheritance, Dr. Midion; his wife, Samantha; and their son, Jarvis, flew from Atlanta to London. It had all been real, not a nightmare at all.

And in London, Siyamon, together with a brutal-looking servant, had tricked Jarvey into coming to his house and standing in front of the Grimoire at the time of its opening. But Siyamon had miscalculated, for when the book drew him into another world, Jarvey had managed to seize it and had kept hold of it. In the strange world called Lunnon, Jarvey had met Betsy Dare, who had helped him survive, and a magician called Zoroaster, who had helped them escape. Zoroaster had told Jarvey that Siyamon had trapped his mother and father in the same way, and now they were somewhere in the Grimoire too—somewhere else, and finding them was going to be hard.

Jarvey and Betsy were in an in-between world, a half-written chapter of the Grimoire, and though they had the book, Zoroaster had warned them that the Grimoire had the dreadful power of enslaving those who used it. Worse, it took a knowledge of magic to use the Grimoire properly. Without that knowledge, Jarvey had no way of controlling which world he would land in whenever he opened the book. The only way to gain mastery of the book was to use it, and using it meant coming under its evil power.

"I'm not sure that's the best thing," Jarvey told Betsy.

She gave a long sigh. "What else is there to do?" she demanded. Betsy had stood by him in Lunnon and had the courage of a lion, but, Jarvey had to admit, she could be really, really annoying at times. Especially when she was right.

"What if we wind up back in Lunnon or something?"

"Been there before, got out of there before. And now His Nibs ain't there, is he?" returned Betsy. "Honestly, if I had any art at all, I'd open that book in a heartbeat!"

"Be glad you didn't inherit it," Jarvey said. Though he and Betsy were remote cousins—her grandfather Zoroaster was a Midion, like Jarvey—she evidently had been born without magic, like Jarvey's father and some others in the family. "All I've got is what old Siyamon called wild magic. Art is magic you control, but with me it just sort of happens—"

6

Sweetly, Betsy said, "If you don't want to find your mum and your dad, that's fine with me."

Jarvey groaned. She was right. They had to use the Grimoire. Jarvey's parents were missing, and he and Betsy couldn't go on without food or water in the gray fog of in-between. "Okay," Jarvey said, his throat still dry. "My parents should be trapped in the last chapter, I think. I'll try for that. Hold my arm." Betsy grabbed hold in a tight grip, and, clenching his teeth, Jarvey spoke the magic word that would unseal the book and let him open it: *"Abrire!"*

He tried to force the book open toward the end of its pages, but the Grimoire seemed to have a will of its own and fought back. Like an animal snapping its jaws, it opened as if to seize him, and a moment later he heard Betsy's shriek as the flipping pages pulled them in, spinning them as if they were in a tornado. It took all Jarvey's strength to hang on as weird lightning flashed and the book yanked him in with the sickening sense of being turned inside out.

2

Passage to Nowhere

Jarvey couldn't even force himself to yell, "Hang on!" He had felt once before the terrible power of the Grimoire, like an amusement-park ride designed by a homicidal maniac. Jarvey had tried to concentrate on finding his parents, but he couldn't keep his mind focused on that, not when the whole world felt as if it were running down a bathtub drain and pulling him with it. He heard a loud clattering and thought, Pages—that's pages turning.

In the next instant, they landed with a crash and tumbled down onto some hard surface. Jarvey had hit hard on his left side. For a few seconds he lay gasping for breath and at last sat up feeling half stunned. "Where are we?" Betsy asked.

"Don't know." He rose and tucked the Grimoire into the front of his shirt. The tall, narrow book was safe there, but it felt strangely heavy.

Jarvey saw dim light all around, a steady faint glow. They had wound up in a long, straight corridor of some kind, made of veiny dark gray marble, floored with mosaic tiles of white and black. It might have been a hallway in a medieval castle, or in a fancy hotel. Candles burning in wall sconces about every twenty feet or so gave some light, and Betsy, always quick to think of what they might need, stood up shakily and plucked one of the candles out of its socket. She stared at it in evident surprise. "Look at this," she told him.

The candle was a fake. Oh, it had a glowing flame and it gave off light, but the flame stayed just the same shape whether you turned the candle on its side or held it upside-down. And it gave off only light, no heat or smoke at all. Jarvey passed his finger through the flame several times and felt nothing.

"We need water," Betsy said. "Then food. Let's go."

Aching from his fall, Jarvey gazed into the distance. The hall stretched both ways as far as they could see. Betsy pointed. "This way's as good as any."

He couldn't disagree with her, and so he trudged along beside her. They walked for what seemed like hours, following the twists and turns of the corridor, occasionally going up short flights of marble stairs, only to emerge in another hallway that looked exactly the same as the first. Betsy kept the candle, though it was of little use. Thousands of other candles stood in the sconces, filling the corridor with a dim yellow light that wore on Jarvey's vision and made his eyelids feel heavy as lead.

"Let's take a break," Jarvey said at last, and Betsy nodded her agreement. He slid down to the cold floor and sat there with his back against the hard marble wall.

"Rum sort of place, this," Betsy grumbled. "Nothing but a kind of long tunnel. Where have you landed us?"

"It wasn't my idea!" snapped Jarvey.

"Maybe it's a maze, like," Betsy said with a thoughtful frown. "Maybe old Siyamon took your mum and dad and stuck them here to wander around forever. Think they'd be sharp enough to leave some clues?"

"With what?" Jarvey asked sarcastically. "There's only the stone walls."

"There's the candles," Betsy pointed out. "I dunno, maybe write on the walls with the wax or something."

"Only there isn't any wax. Look at the candle," he said. "It's not burning down at all."

Betsy turned the candle around and even upside down, but the flame remained constant and the drips and dribbles of wax looked just as they had at the beginning. "Yeah, weird, that." But then Betsy brightened immediately. "Anyway, this tells us that magic's going on here. So we must be in a world some Midion made."

Wonderful, Jarvey thought sourly, a magical, everlasting candle. Great invention of some Midion or other. If it were only edible, it might be of some use.

As if she had read his thought, Betsy complained, "I'm getting really hungry."

"Me too," Jarvey acknowledged. "Ready to go?"

"I'm ready to slenk something to eat," she said in a determined voice.

In Lunnon, Betsy had led an army of street kids, all of them expert at slenking, or stealing, food. There was only one catch. In this maze there didn't seem to be any food to steal.

So they wandered off again, lost in the seemingly endless corridor. They passed no doors at all, and Jarvey lost all track of the turns they took. "I think we're going in circles," he said at last.

"Right," Betsy replied grimly. "Look, can you use your magic to, I dunno, to force there to be a door to go through? To get us outside, some way? Or maybe we could try a different chapter?"

Jarvey gave her an exasperated glance. In the candle-light her copper-red hair gleamed, and the stiff clothes she wore—a gray skirt, a white blouse, and a bonnet—made her look like a character from an old movie. She had donned the clothes to disguise herself as a maid in Tantalus Midion's mansion, and the servant's garments were a far cry from the usual tatters she used to wear. "Look," Jarvey said, "I keep telling you, I don't know how to use the book. I got us here, but if I try again, we may wind up someplace even worse. Let's save that until we get desperate, okay?"

Betsy shrugged. "Come on, then. Somebody made this passageway, so it must go somewhere."

"I wish." But Jarvey cradled the Grimoire and plodded along after her, thinking that this seemed more like a nightmare than his dream of home had.

Jarvey suffered from such dreams often enough. Many times he had experienced things that were, well, strange, even when he was wide-awake. About a year earlier, he had sat in a dentist's chair, needing a small filling but dreading the screaming bite of the whirring drill, and a split second before the drilling began, every piece of electrical equipment in the dentist's office had burned out. Sparks flew, gray smoke puffed out, and the drill seized up and fell silent, leaving Dr. Thornton staring at it in astonishment. Other things like that had happened, especially at moments when Jarvey felt especially tense or excited. Windows had broken for no reason, and a baseball bat had once simply exploded in his hands. After an experience like that, Jarvey always had bad dreams.

In those earlier nightmares he had the power to change things, to make things happen. It was as if his mind were telling him that he had the power, the art, as Siyamon Midion had called it, to do magic. He could change things, transform things, but in his dark dreams, whatever he touched always became monstrous and turned on him.

It took very little for Jarvey's imagination to shift into high gear. What if they came suddenly on the dead, stiff bodies of his mom and dad? Or what if they made the turn and saw Jarvey's parents shuffling toward them, mindless, driven to insanity by the magic of the Grimoire? Or what if this was a world of ghosts—

"Come on!"

Betsy's irritated voice echoed with a hollow sound in the marble corridor. She had taken a lead of twenty feet or so. "What's your hurry?" complained Jarvey, trying to get a grip on his fears. He had begun to dread whatever might lie ahead, but he picked up the pace.

After traveling for what seemed like miles, at least to Jarvey, they finally found a door. Jarvey and Betsy paused before it. It opened off to the left. "Well," Betsy said, "it's something."

Jarvey gave it a dubious inspection. It appeared to be an ordinary door, made of some dark wood, with an ornate brass doorknob and no visible lock. "Yeah," he said. "But what's behind it?" It could be ghosts, his imagination said.

"One way to find out." Betsy reached for the knob.

Jarvey felt himself tensing. "Be careful!"

"Mm." She turned the knob and pushed. The door swung open into a dark room. Cautiously, Betsy held up the candle.

The strain ebbed out of Jarvey. He almost laughed in relief.

"It's a loo," Betsy said. "Thank heavens!"

Jarvey hadn't heard the word loo before coming to London, but since then he had learned that it meant "bathroom." This one looked like the bathroom in a public building: on one wall, a row of three old-fashioned sinks with hand pumps instead of faucets, and beyond them some wooden stalls.

"Me first," Betsy said, sounding as if it was urgent.

Jarvey waited outside the door until she emerged again. "Water tastes all right," she reported. "Wish we had a bottle or something to take some with us."

Taking another candle with him, Jarvey went in and used the bathroom, finally figuring out how to flush. He had to grab a handle dangling from a chain and tug down on it. The water gushed down into the toilet from a big tank up near the ceiling.

He wondered how long it had been since anyone had been in the bathroom. No dust anywhere, but it felt little used, somehow. At least, though, it suggested there were people here, somewhere, if only they could find them. Ghosts didn't need toilets.

At the sink he pumped and gulped some water, quenching his thirst. "Okay," he said, opening the door. "Let's go."

His voice reverberated from the blank wall opposite.

"Hey!" he yelled.

The echo of the word died away, and Jarvey began to get a crawly feeling in the pit of his stomach.

He looked down the corridor to the right. They had

come from that direction, a long, long straight stretch. The marble hallway shrank down in the shadowed distance to nothing. Betsy couldn't have gone that way, or he would see her.

To his left, the corridor went on for a few feet and then took a sudden turn. He went that way, turned the corner, and peered ahead.

The passage led to infinity, or at least to darkness. No one was there.

Like his parents, Betsy had disappeared.

Jarvey was alone.

3

The World's a Stage

"Betsy!" Echoes of Jarvey's voice filled the dim endless hallway, overlapped each other until they faded to an insane murmur. Jarvey gripped his candle and hurried ahead. She wouldn't have turned back, not Betsy. She would have gone straight ahead.

The endless marble corridor was making him feel trapped, claustrophobic. He wanted to run, but run where? It took all of Jarvey's nerve for him to move forward one step at a time, to walk down that strange stone hallway without giving in to blind panic. He had passed no other doors. Where had Betsy gone? How could she have just vanished? He couldn't believe she had left him on purpose. She might be in trouble, might even be—

No. He wouldn't think about what might have happened. That would just get his imagination started, and he'd wind up scaring himself even more. He'd just concentrate on finding her.

But a treacherous thought slowly began to creep into his head. He had the book, the Grimoire, tucked under his left arm. If he had to, he could open the book, speak the spell, and escape from this place. He could escape, but Betsy would have to remain behind.

Then wherever he wound up, he would be alone. But it might be better to be alone, not to have to worry about Betsy, not to have to look out for her—

Where had that thought come from? Betsy had saved his life more than once! She had looked out for him in Lunnon. He couldn't leave her here. Jarvey fought the idea, having the irrational feeling that the Grimoire resented him, that it had a will of its own and was trying to hurt him. The untrustworthy tome could quite easily dump him into someplace even worse than this one, though that was becoming hard for him to imagine.

As his legs grew tired of carrying him, Jarvey forced himself not to whimper. He felt a drumbeat of fear, dread, and uncertainty, keeping time with his slowing steps. He yearned to be out of this strange, shadowy passageway, but Betsy was his friend, and he couldn't just leave her. More, he also knew that he needed help and that Betsy was his most reliable friend. She had stood by him in Lunnon and she had promised to help him find his mom and dad.

So forget the book, he told himself. He couldn't leave his only friend stranded here, in this place, whatever it was.

Walking alone and weary in the dimness, Jarvey had begun to think of one of his father's reference books. It was a big old volume, full of black-and-white photos of relics from the Middle Ages in Europe. One chapter was about the Catacombs of Paris, whole underground streets where the dead lay buried, their dry, dusty bones tumbled on shelves and heaped on the floor. Jarvey couldn't keep one photo out of his mind. It showed a high shelf packed tight with piles and heaps of skulls, their empty eye sockets gazing down at the camera, their fleshless grins seeming to taunt the living. Jarvey had looked at that picture and shivered sometimes, thinking of what it would feel like to be trapped in that dim tomb, stared at by the ranks of the dead. He remembered a poem his class had read, something about an Ancient Mariner. Someone in the poem had walked along a midnight road but didn't dare turn his head because he knew "a fearful fiend did close behind him tread."

The thought made Jarvey even more jumpy, and he continually turned to look back over his shoulder. Jarvey couldn't get rid of the feeling that something stealthy and hidden was trailing him at that moment. The echoes of his own footsteps, though muffled, tricked him into believing feet pattered along behind him. He began to imagine he saw fleeting glimpses of a shadowy form in the dimness far behind, that when he turned around to look, *something* stopped moving off in the distance. He kept thinking if he could twist around quickly enough, he might actually see it move.

Then he looked back once too often, tangled his left foot on his own right ankle, and stumbled, sprawling sideways. His shoulder hit the marble wall on his right—

—and Jarvey felt it give! Rubbing his shoulder, Jarvey reached for the candle he had dropped and held it up. In its steady glow he saw a crack now, the rectangular outline of a doorway. He might have passed a thousand of them without suspecting it, so closely did the marble fit.

And, Jarvey realized, maybe Betsy had made the same discovery! That might account for her sudden disappearance. Jarvey pressed one edge of the door, but only succeeded in closing it. He pushed at the other side, and it tilted open again. This time he got his fingers on the opposite edge and tugged. The door swung open in utter silence, and warm air billowed into his face, air faintly scented with perfume and peppermint. Everything ahead lay in deep darkness, but Jarvey had the impression of a bigger space than the corridor, something like a lobby or an anteroom.

He thought he heard a faint rustling sound. "Betsy?" he said in hardly more than a whisper. "Betsy? Is that you?"

He squinted and saw a dim figure in the gloom ahead. It looked like Betsy, or anyway, it looked like a girl. He held the candle high, but its feeble light didn't reach far enough. "Betsy?" he asked in a louder voice.

"Betsy." The word came back in a sighing, whispery tone that made goose bumps pop up on Jarvey's arms. The figure seemed to beckon. It turned and walked away to the left, into the darkness.

"Wait!" Jarvey hurried after her, and behind him the concealed door silently swung shut. He could barely see in this darkness, but the girl's figure glided away from him, and he followed. It occurred to him that his footsteps were silent now, and glancing down, he saw in the faint circle of light from the candle a carpet of an intricate pattern, red and white, yellow and black, pale blue and deep maroon.

Jarvey heard something ahead and looked up, and his heart leaped. Betsy had stopped just ahead of him. He could see the gleam of her hair and the drab darkness of her servant's dress. "Where did you go?" he demanded, coming up behind her.

She turned, and Jarvey almost dropped the candle. It wasn't Betsy. It wasn't even human.

The face looked like that of an ancient porcelain doll, crisscrossed with lines, with white plastery patches where the surface had flaked away. One eye socket was empty and hollow, with spiderwebs inside, and the other eye was bleary and glazed. Half the nose was gone, broken off, and a big chunk of the left cheek had chipped away, leaving a hole the size of a playing card. Jarvey could see teeth inside.

"Welcome, sir," the thing said in that whispery voice. "My name is Betsy. My name is Linda. My name is Mary. My name is Molly. My name is—" The head jerked, and the thing took a step closer. "May I take take take your hat your coat your stick your your may I thank you you've been a won wonderful aud aud—"

It stumbled, then fell forward. Jarvey jumped backward, and the creature landed flat on its face. It made a sickening crackling sound, and when it tried to push itself up, both of its arms broke at the elbow. Its wobbling head raised up. "Oh sir sir sir I seem to have fallen you are so kind thank thank thank you." No expression in the voice at all, just a crazy whisper, and the remaining eye had fallen out. As the thing jabbered, its bottom jaw flopped wildly and fell off, leaving it looking like a horrible kind of mummy, still trying to talk: "faah haaa awww faah . . . " It tried to drag itself forward on its stumps of arms.

Jarvey couldn't stand it. He turned and ran back into the dark, ran as hard as he could. He turned a corner and stepped onto nothing, rolled, and tumbled down a short carpeted stair.

He scrambled up, frantically reaching for the candle he had dropped, the weird candle that kept on burning. The second he gripped it, he heard something: a distant sound, rising and falling, like waves breaking on a beach.

Jarvey got up, his knees shaking, and saw that he stood in a kind of alcove, curtained off at the opposite side. It was difficult to tell, but in the light of his candle Jarvey thought the curtains looked like rich black velvet, gathered into many draped layers. The sound came from somewhere beyond them. Jarvey started forward and yelped in alarm when a firm hand touched his shoulder.

"No lights in the auditorium," a whispery voice said, and a slim white hand plucked the candle from his grip. The man who had stepped from the darkness might have been made of darkness himself, except for his pale thin face and hands. His features were vaguely aristocratic, a long straight nose and firm chin, but he looked *dead*. Like the girl, he had skin crackled into a thousand zig-zag pieces, and his eyes, a cloudy blue-gray, stared straight ahead in their sockets without moving. He had no chunks missing from his face, but his lips were so white, they looked bloodless. The man's left hand, holding the candle, seemed to be mostly bones, barely covered by a parchment-thin layer of bleached skin.

"This way, sir." With his free hand, the man reached out and parted the black curtains, and Jarvey hurried through the opening.

It wasn't quite as dark, and now he could hear a man's voice trembling in a kind of wail: "Oh, I have lost my love and life! Adieu, my fair, my darling wife. Report how my sad tale ends, report me true, I beg, my friends, that the world at large may know of poor Iacchalus and his tale . . . of woe!"

Then another man's voice: "Alas, he is dead, his spirit fled. His gallant heart has burst from sorrow. Friends, bear him away; we shall pause to judge and say what punishment to give his direst foe tomorrow."

Jarvey came to what felt like a metal railing, and looking ahead he realized that far below him, shrunk to postage-stamp size by distance, a stage lay bathed in light. On it actors who seemed no bigger than ants moved slowly. The light faded as a curtain came down, and then an unseen audience, thousands and thousands of people, began to applaud, crying out, "Bravo!" and "Author!"

"It's a theater!" Jarvey said, feeling both relieved and surprised.

Because it was certainly the largest theater he had ever been in, the largest he could imagine. He stood at the back of an enormous horseshoe-shaped auditorium, with curving banks of seats falling away before him, down to that far-off stage.

The curtain rose again, and in the spill of light from it Jarvey could just make out the actors, bowing to the applause. That was what had sounded like surf! They took bow after bow, and then one stepped forward to an ovation like thunder. The sound very gradually died down, and then the man who had been acting the part of Iacchalus said, "Thank you, kind friends, thank you. Now that we have given you a tale of sadness and tragedy, we shall lift your spirits next time with a comedy. Our next performance, I am pleased to say, will be one of your old favorites, the happy story of the four foolish lovers and their equally foolish families, newly augmented with striking original scenes and three new songs. Please return to see our humble offering of *The Lovers' Stratagem, or, Two Couples Uncoupled*. Good night!"

The curtain fell for the last time on the stage, but now chandeliers dangling on long chains were creaking down from high openings in the ceiling, and a warm yellow wash of candlelight streamed from them, illuminating the crowd below. Jarvey had never seen so many people assembled in one place in his whole life, not at football games, not anywhere. The men all wore dark evening clothes, long black coats, white shirts, white ties, and top hats, and the women wore a rainbow of old-fashioned evening gowns, shimmering blues and reds. The men and women alike murmured as they turned to leave, all of them sounding very pleased with the play they had just seen. Jarvey caught fragments of their comments: *Splendid voice . . . moved to tears . . . another triumph . . . glorious, glorious.*

Jarvey dodged aside as a torrent of people made their

way up the slanting aisles toward the passages he had just left. Nobody seemed to notice him as he stared up at the passing throng. All around the auditorium, crowds of men and women poured into the aisles. Jarvey gawped at them because he felt vaguely bothered by something. Lots of the people looked very much alike. There were about half a dozen different models of men, half a dozen models of women. All the men with dark mustaches looked enough alike to be brothers, if not twins. All the blond women in dark dresses were nearly identical, and so it was with the other models as well. And the conversations repeated themselves too. For twenty or thirty times, Jarvey heard identical-looking men tell identical-looking women, "We must come back for the comedy. I know you'll enjoy it."

Finally the last few straggling people walked past him, and as they left through the black velvet curtains and stepped into the dark passageway, a sudden silence fell. Jarvey brought up the rear of the group. He ducked through the curtain and stopped in his tracks, feeling the hairs on his arms prickling.

The old man who had taken his candle stood alone, like a statue. No one else was in the passageway. But it should have been jammed! The audience members hadn't had time to go anywhere.

They had vanished the same way Betsy had disappeared, seemingly into thin air. They seemed to have faded away, like—well, like ghosts.

Jarvey somehow didn't want to follow them out into the darkness. He turned back and reentered the auditorium. In the helpful light of the chandeliers, he found a long aisle and walked down it, toward the stage. The auditorium was so huge that, looking up, he couldn't even see the ceiling at its highest point. The chandeliers seemed to be dangling down from infinity.

As he passed row after row of seats, Jarvey noticed something else. The carpeted floor and aisles lay clean, cleaner than any theater he had ever seen. No scrap of litter lay anywhere, and the seats all had been neatly folded up. After walking for what felt like a mile, he reached the front of the theater and only then did he realize how large the stage actually was. It was a lot bigger than his front yard back home, and the set on it looked gigantic. It represented a street in some city, vaguely reminding Jarvey of pictures he had seen of ancient Rome. Substantial three-storied marble-fronted houses, their fronts decorated with stone columns, formed the backdrop. A fountain in the center of the stage featured mermaids and soldiers in armor, and from a central column it jetted real water in a gurgling spray.

Separating the stage from the auditorium was a deep U-shaped pit with chairs arranged in orderly rows. It might have been the orchestra pit, Jarvey supposed, though he hadn't heard any music accompanying the play. No steps led down into the pit from the auditorium, but the drop wasn't all that great. He clambered over the low brass railing, let himself down until he dangled a few feet off the ground, and then released his grip, falling the last little distance.

His landing made a sharp thump, but no one seemed to be around to hear it. He found a metal ladder fixed to the back wall of the pit, and it allowed him to climb up onto the stage.

Jarvey stood blinking for a moment. Bright light streamed in from somewhere, though he couldn't spot its source. The radiance bathed everything on stage, though. He walked to the center of the platform and to his surprise saw that the realistic fountain was simply a flat cardboard cutout. Pale blue streamers blew in a jet of air. He had thought it was real water, but from up close he could see that it was not only fake, but sort of shabby-looking too. How had something like that fooled him?

And now he could see that the three-dimensional street of Romanesque houses was simply a flat painting as well.

It didn't look convincing at all from here, although from far away he would have sworn that it was real.

Jarvey cautiously explored the left side of the stage, stepping into the wings. A wilderness of taut ropes and stacked weights cluttered the wall there, and a curtained-off doorway led to what seemed to be a row of a dozen dressing rooms, all of them empty. Long tables stood against walls lined with mirrors. Empty chairs had been thrust back away from the tables. A faint scent a little like the waxy aroma of crayons hung in the air.

The last dressing room, and the grandest, was a little different, though. A table in the center of this one held a silver bowl, and the bowl held some withered fruit, pears and apples. They weren't fresh and they certainly weren't crisp, but Jarvey devoured every bite of them.

He drank too, from an old-fashioned sink in that room. He noticed a long rack hung with a couple of dozen costumes, wrinkling his nose at the smell of stale sweat hanging over the outfits. On the long tables before the mirrors, wig stands without faces gazed at him balefully. When he moved up and down the length of the makeup table, he had the sense that the wig stands silently turned to keep him in sight.

Rummaging around on the cluttered tabletop, he found

cakes of theatrical makeup, sponges, bottles of lotions and jars of creams, and a few stubby pencils—eyebrow pencils, he supposed. He took one of these, and he took one of those ever-burning candles from a wall sconce outside the dressing room.

In its pale yellow light, he could see a bulletin board hung over with hundreds of pieces of paper. Inspecting them, Jarvey found lists of actors and parts for hundreds of plays. He didn't recognize a single title: *The Roman's Revenge; Hearts in Conflict; Rollo's Seaside Holiday; The Sorrowful History of King Harold; The Play of Ghosts and Shadows;* others by the dozen. Some of the papers looked fresh and crisp, but many others had curled and yellowed with age.

Jarvey pulled four or five of the playbills down from the board, choosing ones that had been concealed by layers of later ones. The backs of the lists were blank. He had a pencil, and now he had paper. Maybe he could leave notes for Betsy. Maybe she would find them and then find Jarvey again.

After all, if she had stumbled into a doorway opening off that maddening corridor, she just might wind up here. Come to that, Jarvey thought, she might even have found her way out of this odd theater, if it had a way out.

He shivered, remembering how the crowd of people

had abruptly, impossibly, evaporated into thin air. How the doll-creature had shattered and yet had tried to drag itself after him with its crumbling arms, crawling over its own fallen jaw.

Jarvey's imagination was racing again. What if the theater wasn't real at all? What if the people were spirits, what if . . .

What if it was all just a theater of ghosts and shadows?

4

Merely Players

*H*ours of searching led Jarvey to only one discovery. He opened a door backstage and found himself in the same corridor he and Betsy had started in. There was the door to the loo, just opposite. If Betsy had stumbled onto this doorway, she had stepped right into the shadows behind the stage. And what had happened to her?

Jarvey knew she was resourceful, quick and smart. He told himself she could get out of any trouble, that she could handle danger. He couldn't help smiling when he remembered how, back in Lunnon, Betsy was such an expert thief that she could steal food right off the table without anyone's noticing. She'd be all right on her own. She didn't really need him to help her survive. Still, he needed her, and he didn't know what he would do if he couldn't find her again.

The Grimoire knew. It whispered to him to open the book, to get out of here, to leave her behind.

"No," he said to himself, not to the Grimoire. That was one thing he couldn't do. But he was tired. He found a place to hide, crept into it, and curled up to grab what sleep he could.

A stranger haunted his dreams, a man with thin arms and a bloated face, an evil face. In all the dreams, Jarvey hid from the man, and the stranger searched for him, swiveling his head, his eyes glaring. The dreams took place nowhere that Jarvey could identify, just shadowy landscapes. And in each dream, the evil man seemed to come a little closer. In the last, Jarvey seemed to be standing behind a tall chain-link fence, like the one on the baseball field where his team played. He heard the links jangling, and looked off into the distance to see the dark-suited man clinging to the opposite side of the fence, creeping along like a human spider, his white face turning from side to side as he looked for Jarvey.

Jarvey woke with a gasp and then realized it was just

another nightmare. He took a few deep breaths, turned on his side, and hung in that warm, drowsy place between sleep and awareness, wondering who the man in those disturbing dreams could be. He had the strangest feeling that he should have recognized the face, yet—

A voice from outside his hiding place broke into his thoughts: "Now remember, all, the key with comedy is to keep it moving fast and believe in your parts. You must never show that you think the play is funny. Leave that to the audience."

Two younger voices said in chorus, "Yes, Father."

Jarvey crawled out from where he had dozed, beneath a row of seats halfway back from the stage, and risked a peek. The Roman street had vanished, and in its place was a set that looked like the deck of a sailing ship. At this distance the illusion struck Jarvey as uncannily real: The masts reared up, the ropes and shrouds ran up to the yard-arms, and the sails billowed and fluttered in what seemed like a salty ocean breeze.

More than a dozen people stood on the deck. The leader seemed to be a tall, strongly built man in the uniform of a sea captain. He was talking to the others: a woman who looked as if she were about the man's age, forty or so, a young man of about eighteen and a girl who might have been a year or so younger, and a semicircle of men and women who seemed strangely quiet and motionless, like a row of department-store dummies. The man said, "Very well. Let us begin with the first scene of Act Two. Floriel and Yolanda have taken passage upon my ship, not realizing that I am the father of Isidor. Isidor has disguised his sweetheart Mariane as a young sailor, and no one knows this except for the countess. Places, please."

The semicircle of immobile actors came to life then, moving across the stage, some going into the wings, others taking their places at the ship's wheel or on the deck. A couple climbed up into the rigging. Peering through the crack between two seats, Jarvey watched the rehearsal with a growing sense of puzzlement. The actors seemed to anticipate laughter from their audience because they often paused in their lines or in their actions, but as far as Jarvey was concerned, nothing was terribly funny.

Finally, the captain said, "And then curtain, the interval, and we're into Act Three. Very good. It is time for lunch, and after lunch we shall finish Acts Three and Four. Thank you, all." He put his arm around the waist of the woman who had played the part of the countess. "A grand performance, as usual, my dear," he said.

She giggled. "And you were wonderful as well. Your gifts truly shine, Mr. Midion."

Jarvey gasped at the name and felt like drawing his head back, like a turtle retreating into its shell. If the actor was a Midion, then this strange theater must be his creation, from his part of the book. As the cast all trooped offstage, Jarvey slipped out of his hiding place and hurried down to the front. The last thing he wanted was to follow the actors, but that was exactly what he had to do.

He dropped into the orchestra pit as quietly as he could manage, then climbed the metal ladder onto the stage. The actors had gone off in the direction of the dressing rooms. He stepped into the dark wings of the theater and heard a loud laugh coming from the last dressing room, the one down on the far end of the row.

Jarvey ducked sideways through another open doorway just in time. The young man who had played the role of Floriel came out of and walked away from the last dressing room and disappeared down a hallway. Jarvey sighed in relief at not having been noticed.

And then he turned around and almost yelped in surprise. Six women sat rigidly in six chairs at the makeup table, all of them staring silently at their reflections. "I'm sorry," Jarvey said in a hoarse voice. "I didn't know—" he broke off. Not one of the actresses had turned to look at him, had even seemed to notice him. The one nearest him had played the role of Yolanda. She sat like a statue, as did the others. Jarvey couldn't even see them breathe.

He cautiously approached Yolanda. She didn't stir, didn't move a muscle, didn't even turn toward him when he stood at her shoulder. "Hello?" he said. He waved his hand in front of her face. She did not even blink. Jarvey gulped and thought back to the rehearsal, remembering one of the many unfunny jokes. He gave the actress her cue: "Oh, Yolanda! Your father is a hard man!"

Immediately her dead face came to life in a simpering smile, and in exactly the same tone she had used earlier onstage, she said, "No wonder, for in his youth he was a stone mason." That said, she froze again, placidly staring at her own face in the mirror.

Close up, Jarvey could see there was something not right about her. Her skin was too smooth, too pink at the cheeks. She looked more like a life-sized doll than a person. She was like a newer version of the terrible crumbling, creeping thing that he had mistaken for Betsy. "Are you some kind of robot?" Jarvey asked.

The actress did not answer.

Jarvey backed away. He checked to make sure the coast

was clear and slipped into the next dressing room, where half a dozen men sat staring into their own mirror. Jarvey could recognize them from the rehearsal. One was young Isidor, the sweetheart of Mariane. Another was old Bellibone, Yolanda's father. They were just as lifeless as Yolanda had been.

But in the last dressing room, matters were different. Jarvey didn't dare get close enough to peek in, but the door stood ajar and he could hear voices.

"Excellent sandwiches, Mrs. Midion."

"Thank you, Mr. Midion."

"I wish Augustus would come with the tea!"

"Patience, my dove. Your brother will be back soon."

"He's always such a slowpoke, Father. I don't see why we can't have a nice little place for making tea right here in our dressing room."

"Honoria, you know quite well that a home is a home," the woman who had played the countess said in a firm voice, "and the theater is the theater. We do not perform in our living room, and so we shall not cook in our dressing room."

Honoria grumbled that tea wasn't really cooking, but Jarvey heard only a little of her complaint, because he had retreated into the men's dressing room, where he could peek out from reasonably good concealment, and before long he saw the younger man returning, carrying a teapot and a basket. "Father," he said as he entered the last dressing room, "I have the strangest feeling that someone has been in our kitchen."

The older man's voice broke into a laugh. "Hardly any chance of that, Augustus! Now, boy, you can get a much bigger laugh on your exit line—yes, pour the tea, do."

Jarvey bit his lip to keep himself from laughing in relief. He could guess who had been in their kitchen, all right. Someone who was an expert at snitching food right out from under the noses of its proper owner.

It had to be Betsy.

5

Master of the World

*B*etsy slipped out of the cupboard where she had folded herself up into an astonishingly small space, getting her breath back again. The boy had almost caught her.

She had been munching a slice of bread spread with a little honey, and she finished her sticky meal as she made her way out of the apartment. For about the hundredth time she wondered how she was going to find Jarvey again. Ever since she had discovered the secret doorway in the corridor wall, she had been moving through this endless building. Strange, she had been sure that Jarvey was right behind her at first. She had heard his footsteps following her when she first came out into the darkness that filled the backstage of a huge theater, but when she turned, he wasn't there at all. Worse, she'd heard people approaching, and before she'd found her bearings, she'd had to scuttle away, hiding from them. Now she had no idea of where the doorway back to the marble corridor was, just that it must be one of the dozens in the backstage part of the theater.

"Doesn't matter," she told herself, wiping her sticky fingers on the hem of her dress. "Jarvey will have to wind up in the theater sooner or later."

Because that's all there was.

Betsy was convinced of it. She had explored for hours, and so far as she could tell, this whole world consisted of the apartment kept by the actors of the Midion family, their small backyard garden (not that it was really so small to someone from crowded Lunnon), and all the rest of it was taken up in long corridors surrounding that enormous auditorium.

Once she'd had a look around, Betsy's sense of direction was unerring. From the apartment she turned away from the direction leading to the stage and followed a short hallway down to the garden door. It had no lock. In

fact, there were none on any of the doors here. She supposed that the father of the acting family, or maybe the
mother, was the one who had created this world, and he or
she would be sure that no enemies were in it. No enemies,
no need for locks. Not like Lunnon, she thought, where
no one quite trusted anyone else.

She opened the door and slipped into the garden, glad
for a sight of the sun. She stood on what seemed to be the
floor of a kind of rectangular crater. Except for the one
door, the marble walls rose up from the soil unbroken on
all sides. Terrace on terrace reared all around, each one a
little more set back than the one it rested on.

The garden was all the greenery in this whole world,
as far as she could tell. It might have stretched a mile or
a mile and a half on a side. A little stream meandered
through it, rising from a mound of stone in one corner
and running to a pool in the opposite corner. One whole
section grew thick with pear and apple trees, and other
areas had been planted with grains, vegetables, and some
plants Betsy could not recognize.

She had hidden in the orchard earlier that day and
watched the four members of the Midion family come
out to pick vegetables and to rehearse songs. At first she
had wondered how this garden, big as it was, could pos-

sibly support a whole population, but gradually she had come to realize that these four *were* the whole population. The other actors and actresses, the audiences, were all illusions, conjured up by the Midion magic. None of them were real. The actors were some kind of walking, talking dolls, and the audience members were more like spirits or ghosts.

And you don't need to eat or drink if you're only a doll or a ghost.

But Betsy was neither, so she ate some fruit, then slipped back through the only door leading out of the garden. She made her way through the dim hallways until she heard the actors rehearsing their parts out on stage. She peeked inside the first dressing room, found it empty, and scavenged a few remnants from the actors' meal. Wherever Jarvey was, she hoped he was not starving.

About forty feet away, Jarvey crouched in the women's dressing room. Only one of the actresses remained there, apparently waiting for some cue. Jarvey tried talking to her and found that she, like the other woman, would do two things: recite her lines if given the right lead-in line and talk about the theater. Now, in an urgent whisper, he asked, "But just what is this theater?"

The actress-doll turned her glassy eyes toward him. Prettily, she chirped, "The world is a theater. The theater is a world!" And she giggled, but then looked distressed until Jarvey softly clapped his hands.

He had figured out that applause was the key. The strange actors and actresses would speak, in their fashion, as long as you rewarded them by clapping. They seemed to be hungry for that sign of approval. The doll-creature daintily inclined her head in a symbolic bow.

"Listen, have you seen a girl?" he asked.

The actress-doll did not answer. "Her name is Betsy," he added urgently. "She has really red hair, a lot redder than mine—"

He broke off as another actress-doll, an older woman, came into the room and took her place at the end of the long makeup table. She was murmuring something softly, echoing what Jarvey had just said: "Redder than mine. Give me wine," she said in a low, despairing voice, "wine as red as a young woman's lips, and redder still than mine. Let me drink of it, as I drink of sorrow." A tear rolled down her right cheek.

Jarvey resignedly clapped for her, and she thanked him with a little smile and a slight bob of her chin. He muttered, "Well, thanks for nothing, anyway."

He edged past her and peeked out, but no one stood in the wings. Onstage the actors, both the real ones and the doll-things, were singing heartily, a song with a lot of "Yo-ho's" in it and a lot of high soprano trills from the ladies.

Maybe if he went the other way, went down the hallway where the boy had gone to fetch the tea—

Jarvey opened the door and whooped in alarm, and a hand clapped over his mouth at once. Betsy grabbed his wrist and hauled him down a long corridor. "Come on!" she growled. "You'll have them all on us, cully!"

They pounded out a door and into dazzling sunlight.

Jarvey blinked, not daring to believe his eyes. "You found the way out!"

"Don't wave the flag yet. Come on, duck down low and get into the wheat—no, you goose, the wheat, the tall grassy stuff! Lower!"

She put a hand on his back and forced him to lie on his stomach, while she hugged the ground next to him. A moment later, the door they had come through opened again, and the older man and the boy stepped out. "Nothing," the man said. "Augustus, what is the matter with you? You know that an actor should never break character—"

"I heard someone call out," Augustus doggedly insisted. "I know I did, Father."

The man looked at his son for a long time, shaking his head.

Jarvey's breathing was painful, because inside his shirt the Grimoire pressed hard against his chest, and he was trying to push himself right down into the dirt. If the two looked the right way, they'd spot him for sure, he thought, wishing he had chosen a spot with better cover. Betsy was more well hidden than he, with tall clumps of wheat growing all around her. Jarvey lay more or less between rows.

However, neither of the two figures glanced his way. The older actor sighed and said, "Oh, I don't know. Perhaps you did hear something at that. Katrina Three has been behaving oddly these past few months, missing cues, even ad-libbing laughter now and again. Perhaps it's time I retired her to become an usher and created a replacement."

"I don't think it was her."

The older man clapped the younger one on the shoulder in a fatherly gesture. "She, my boy. The proper way of saying it is 'I don't think it was she.'"

Jarvey could see Augustus's expression, and from it he judged that Augustus didn't much care what the proper way of saying it was. He looked angry and a little dangerous, as if he wanted to hit something, anything.

"Come back inside, son," the father said, holding his hand out. "We must return to our rehearsal." He patted the boy on the back, and they both disappeared through the door.

As soon as they were gone, Jarvey sat up. "What happened to you?" he asked. "I looked everywhere!"

"Stay down!" Betsy clamped a hand on his neck and pushed him so he lay on his side, hidden by the wheat. "I found a door that led backstage," she said before he could speak. "I thought you were right behind me! I heard—"

"I thought I saw you—"

They stared at each other for a moment, and then they both laughed. It was a shaky, nervous kind of laugh, but still a relief. "Those dolls," Betsy said. "They wear out or something, and then—"

"He makes new ones," Jarvey said. "The old ones get put out in the hallways and just sort of wander around until"—he shivered—"until they fall apart."

"'S good to see you," Betsy said. "You had enough to eat?"

"Some."

"Get more out here. Lots of lovely fruits and things.

Water too, not bad. D'you think your mom and dad are here?"

Jarvey shook his head. "I don't think so. I don't know for sure, though. Look, do me a favor, and don't go off by yourself again. I don't like being on my own."

"Missed you too, cully," she said with a shy grin. "But what is this place? A whole world that's just a theater? Who are these people?"

To answer her, Jarvey raised up on his elbow and reached into his shirt, where he had stuck the playbills along with the Grimoire. He pulled out a handful of them. "Look at these."

The first one, in very ornate lettering, was like all the rest except in a few details:

The Unparalleled Tragedy of Horatius

or

MASTER OF THE WORLD

By Mr. Junius Midion
Directed by Mr. Junius Midion
Featuring Mr. Junius Midion
as "Horatius"
With the Added Talents of

Mr. Augustus Midion
Miss Honoria Midion
And the Most Beloved Actress on
This or Any Stage,
Mrs. Sarah Midion,
wife of Mr. Junius Midion

Betsy leafed through the playbills, shaking her head, as Jarvey told her about seeing the crumbling creature in the corridor, the mysterious vanishing audience, and about the bizarre actor-dolls he had found in the dressing rooms. "I don't think anyone but the family is even really alive here," he finished. "They've turned this world into a theater where they're always the stars."

"That's crazy," Betsy responded. "It's like playacting when you're little children. If no one is real except the Midion family, if there's no real audience, then what's the point?"

"I don't know," Jarvey admitted. A stray, bent stalk of wheat was tickling his neck. "Do you think we might get up now?"

"Well, perhaps," Betsy said. "They seem to have gone. Maybe we should wait a bit, though."

But Jarvey was tired of lying down, with the Grimoire

uncomfortable against his chest. "It's okay. Come on." He stood up and began to dust himself off.

And at that moment the door, not a hundred feet from him, banged open and Augustus Midion stared straight at Jarvey with angry eyes and shouted, "Father! Father! Come quickly!"

6

Walking Shadows

Jarvey dropped to his knees, thrust the Grimoire into Betsy's hands, and said, "He hasn't seen you! Keep it safe!" Then he leaped up and bolted, running for the orchards at the far side of the garden.

Jarvey sprinted full-tilt, arms pumping. He circled away so that if Augustus was pursuing him he wouldn't notice Betsy, but after a few hundred feet he realized he *wasn't* being pursued. He leaped over a winding pebble-lined brook and then risked a glance behind him. At the far end of the mile-long garden, the door stood open, but he couldn't see anyone standing in the doorway, and no one in the garden, unless Augustus was crouching, staring at him from the wheat or the rows of beans. Betsy was nowhere to be seen, and if the coast was clear, she'd be heading for him.

Jarvey couldn't take the chance that Augustus wasn't somewhere out in the garden. He ducked down and hustled, taking a zigzag course. Sweat stung his eyes, and his chest began to ache from effort. Finally, in the shade of a triple row of apple trees, he had to pause to get his breath. He ducked behind a tree, stood up, and craned cautiously to look out. Still no sign of pursuit. Had Augustus and his father trapped Betsy?

No, Jarvey told himself, that wasn't likely. Bets was far too experienced at evading capture. He knew how she could find cover, how she could all but make herself invisible. She didn't share the magical abilities of her grandfather, the mysterious Zoroaster, though. Jarvey remembered vividly how Zoroaster had once briefly turned both of them invisible, and how Jarvey was blind during the spell because his invisible eyes could not focus light on his invisible retinas. Betsy had no magic like that, but she was an experienced thief and she must have gotten away. She might even have sneaked inside the building and might be making her way back to—

Jarvey shrank behind the gnarled black trunk of one of the trees, his hand gripping the rough bark. Augustus had just stepped outside the door, and with him his father. The two distant, tiny figures seemed to be arguing, though from this far away Jarvey could see very little of them and could hear nothing at all.

He backed away until he came to the last and biggest tree, growing right up against the bare marble wall. Jarvey stretched to grasp the lowest limb, grabbed hold of it, and swung himself up. He crept higher in the tree, hauling himself from limb to limb to a place where leaves concealed him well, but where there was a little tunnel through the leaves that let him see the garden. The branches hung heavy with masses of fragrant apple blossoms, and if Jarvey hadn't been so scared and exhausted, he might actually have enjoyed the climb, except maybe for the bees.

Golden honeybees buzzed all around him, and from this height he could see rows of square white wooden beehives in a long line against the marble wall over to his left. Jarvey fanned with his hand, trying to discourage the honeybees from investigating his sweaty face. They were real insects, not illusions. Jarvey supposed the Midions needed them to pollinate the garden, and maybe to produce honey—wait, something was going on out there, something moving slowly toward him like a spread-out, gray mist.

Jarvey gasped and scrunched himself small. Walking through the rows of crops, still far away but coming toward him, stalked a whole row of men in dark evening dress. Junius Midion must have summoned members of his phantom audience to join in the search. At the very center of the line, Junius and Augustus strode along, peering this way and that. Where was Bets? He couldn't see her. He hoped she'd found a place to hide. If Junius Midion got his hands on the Grimoire . . .

But right now he had to worry about being caught himself. Jarvey desperately looked around for some means of escape. He had none. The tree was too far away from the next one for him to move over. He couldn't climb down without the risk of being spotted.

But perhaps he could climb higher! This was one of the tallest of the apple trees, and its old, twisted branches thrust up and up and then spread out in all directions. It might be just possible, Jarvey thought, to swing out onto a branch and reach the roof of the first terrace.

He climbed slowly, inches at a time, not wanting to draw attention to himself and not trusting the old branches to hold him. At one point a curious bee landed on his face. Jarvey froze and felt the maddening itch as the insect crawled over his forehead, down his closed eyelid, and across his right cheek before taking off and buzzing away. Staying still and keeping quiet for that was about the hardest thing that Jarvey had ever done.

The higher limbs were smaller and less sturdy. Jarvey found one that crooked out and overhung the terrace, and he swung his way out on that one, hand over hand, with his feet dangling, but the old wood creaked as though in warning, and the branch began to bend and shake. A few leaves fell spinning from the smaller twigs.

With an effort, Jarvey got himself just far enough out and, stretching down, stood on tiptoe on the flat roof of the marble terrace, still gripping the branch. He released his hold carefully, letting the limb swoosh back up into place as slowly and quietly as possible. The marble underfoot had collected years of fallen apple-tree leaves, and these had decayed into a kind of mushy, slippery soil. Jarvey edged his way out of this mess and onto the smooth bare stone, backing and crouching at the same time. The ghostly searchers had walked more than halfway across the garden by then. If only they wouldn't look up, Jarvey thought, he might be safe. However, from this point he couldn't see much of the garden at all, except for the tops of the trees, and so he was out of sight of the searchers.

The sinking sun beat down, so fierce that its heat felt almost like a physical pressure on his skin. After what seemed like an hour, he heard voices, first just the murmurous sound, and then the actual words. Junius Midion seemed angry. "You have interrupted our precious rehearsal time for this, my son. Well, here we are, and there is no boy. Augustus, are you satisfied at last that you were mistaken?"

Augustus sounded dogged and upset when he replied, "I know I saw him, Father. A little ragamuffin of twelve or thirteen, a lot like Bates in *Life on the Streets, or, The Beggars' Tragedy.*"

"But we haven't done that play in thirty or forty seasons now, and we haven't had a Bates in ages," Junius shot back. "Nor a boy of twelve or thirteen in any of our plays of late date."

Jarvey lay on his stomach and inched forward. He peeked over the edge of the terrace and saw Junius and Augustus nearly below him, under the shade of the trees. Beyond them, the phantom army of searchers wavered in the sunlight, looking transparent and insubstantial. None of them thought to look up.

From twenty feet below Jarvey, Junius Midion chuckled, a rich, self-satisfied sound. "Son, I think I know what is happening. You have a wonderful imagination, the great Midion gift of invention, and it is acting up a bit just at present. Like your father, you are destined to be a great playwright as well as a talented and successful actor. Perhaps your first effort might be titled *The Ghost Boy, or, The Intruder in the Garden*, eh?"

Augustus nearly snarled, "Don't make fun of me, Father! I know what I saw."

"My boy, those of us who have become celebrated on the stages of the world—"

This time Augustus sounded positively angry with his father: "Celebrated? Father, they used to laugh at your tragedies and boo at your comedies! Until you used the Grimoire to create the World Theater, no one appreciated your plays or our acting!"

"They were fools," Junius said coldly. "Fools and philistines, who had no true understanding of the muses of comedy and tragedy! The greater their loss when we left them behind forever. I'm surprised you think of them at all, boy, after so much time has passed, after their idiotic disapproval has been swamped with the love and adoration our audiences here have shown us for our efforts. This is much better. Now we have audiences who understand us, who always applaud! Don't you agree, all of you?"

Even though the hot sun was wringing sweat from him, Jarvey felt a chill pass down his spine as a chorus of low, whispery voices began to rustle like wind in the trees: "Astonishing performance, sir!" "Excellently well written!" "Very moving!" "I've never laughed so much!" The voices died down gradually to a distant hum and then to silence. Though the words were enthusiastic, the tone of the voices sounded infinitely sad and dreary to Jarvey.

"Could there be anyone in the trees?" Augustus demanded in a peevish sort of way. "If he got this far, surely he'd think to climb."

Jarvey ducked back.

"Look up," Junius ordered. "Look carefully. Is there a boy concealed in the trees, my friends?"

Again came the chorus of weirdly identical voices: "No, sir." "Nothing, sir." "I see no one, sir."

Augustus was not satisfied. "Maybe I should climb up in one of them just to make sure. If he got this far, he might have—"

Then Junius sighed. "Come on, son. We really have no time for this just at present. I want to finish with Act Four today, so tomorrow we can concentrate on the grand climax and of course our curtain call. Remember, we perform on the evening after that."

"But Father—"

"Augustus, if it makes you feel better, I shall place a spell of warning on the garden and on all the doors. There cannot be an intruder, for where would he come from? But if anything is out of place or wrong, we shall know instantly just where it is and what it is."

"A spell will take you hours."

"After our rehearsal, I shall attend to it, Augustus," Junius said firmly. "Come."

Jarvey heard retreating footsteps, and again he wormed his way forward on his stomach until he could peek over the edge of the terrace.

What he saw startled him so much that he almost overbalanced and fell off the edge of the flat roof. The whole row of top-hatted, black-coated men stood directly beneath him, about a foot away from the wall, facing the wall and staring straight ahead at the marble. Junius and Augustus were striding away through the bean rows some distance away, heading for the distant doorway.

But the strange thing was that the men underneath him were *dissolving*. Their top hats were already transparent when Jarvey first caught sight of them, and in a few seconds they had disappeared. And then, horribly, the flesh and hair crept away from their heads, starting at the crown, revealing translucent, milky skulls that almost immediately grew as clear as glass and then vanished in shreds of gray vapor. The necks, the shoulders, the arms, the chests all faded to skeletal bones, and then the bones evaporated like mist in the sun. The whole process might have taken no more than ten seconds, but to Jarvey it seemed to stretch on and on.

Even after the ghostly men had disappeared, Jarvey didn't dare to come down for a long time. Far across the garden the forms of Junius and Augustus slipped inside the doorway. From here Jarvey could not even tell for sure that they had closed the door. With great caution he crept sideways, into the shade of the tree, and waited.

At last, as the sun slanted lower in the cloudless sky, Jarvey stood up, walked out into the mushy layer of leaf mold, and made a leap straight upward. With hands already sore and blistered from his earlier climb, he caught the creaking branch and hauled himself into the apple tree again. He worked his way down, dropped to the ground, and began to search for Betsy. He couldn't find her anywhere, and at last he limped toward the only doorway out of the garden. His leg muscles felt stiff and sore, and his throat felt parched. From a safe distance he could see the door was indeed shut.

He hoped it wasn't locked.

Like a flat lid sliding over the top of a square box, a gray layer of cloud had swept in from behind him, shutting off the direct sunlight. Jarvey soon heard the patter of rain, then felt the first drops as he crossed the little winding brook in the center of the garden.

He shivered. Even the rain was spooky, more like water drizzling from regularly spaced sprinklers than real rain. He wondered if Junius had arranged the weather on this odd world so that his garden would be watered every afternoon. Lunnon had experienced occasional storms, but Tantalus Midion, who had created that world, had not paid as much attention to detail as Junius. Lunnon had not even had a proper sun, just a diffuse, brassy glow in the sky. But Lunnon had people in it, real people, criminals whom Tantalus had brought to his world, kidnap victims whom he had taken by force, and their descendants, real flesh-and-blood people, not ghosts and robots. There the people were substantial, and the buildings had been made by their hands, not by magic. The weather in Lunnon and the surroundings was random and messy. Here everything seemed somehow sharp, substantial—everything but the people.

But then, Junius probably was the one who had designed and created all the stage sets with their amazing impression of reality. Why should his world look false when he was such a master of illusion?

Jarvey reached the door at last, soaked to the skin and miserable, and tried the handle. It opened immediately.

Jarvey tiptoed down the hallway, and as he was passing a darkened doorway, someone inside went "Psst!" making him jump about a foot.

"It's me," Betsy hissed from the darkness. "Here's where they live!"

Jarvey ducked inside the doorway. First he passed through an alcove, then into a cluttered room thickly furnished with overstuffed chairs, sofas, and love seats. Colored-pencil sketches of Junius, Augustus, Honoria, and Sarah Midion almost covered every wall in the room, the pictures showing their subjects in various theatrical costumes: pirates, soldiers, ancient Greeks and Romans, and kings, queens, princesses, and princes. With a rush of relief, Jarvey saw that Betsy had laid the Grimoire on a table. On top of it she had opened a large scrapbook. "Look at this," she said.

The pages seemed very old, yellowed and brittle with age. Pasted in the scrapbook were dozens of newspaper and magazine stories, all about Junius and Sarah Midion. Some were dated. Jarvey saw one that came from the year 1822.

All of the articles were reviews of plays that the Midions had done back on the real Earth. Jarvey didn't have to read many to understand that Junius Midion's reputation as actor and playwright had been pretty miserable back in those days. The kindest of them said one of the plays was "not actually completely foul."

"According to these, they're all horrible actors," Betsy said.

Jarvey told her what he had overheard in the garden. "I was right," he finished. "Junius Midion got hold of the Grimoire and used its magic to build a world where everyone would always love him and his family. Now he can make up any play at all, and it's always a hit." He reached for the Grimoire, and Betsy, who never liked to be close to the book, shivered a little. "Come on, we've got to get out of here. Maybe we can leave tonight, when the family's asleep. But we can't let them catch us in their apartment."

"But your mother and father—"

"I don't think they could be here in this world," Jarvey said. "When Siyamon Midion tried to trap me in the book, he told me to turn to the very last chapter. This can't be the last chapter in the book. It must've been written even before the Lunnon one you came from, because the date's earlier. When I tried to use the Grimoire, we went the wrong way. Siyamon would probably put my mom, my dad, and me in the chapter he was writing, not just stick them somewhere else in the book. Come on. Let's get someplace where we know we'll be safe and I'll open the Grimoire and get us out of here."

They followed the hall to the backstage of the theater. The whole group of actors and actresses, real and artificial, seemed to be out on the stage, singing a very loud song that didn't even rhyme very well:

Oh, our lovers face much woe,
And they don't know where to go,
For the world seems turned against the four of them;
Will they find the way
To a new and brighter day,
And will their parents pay,
We cannot just now say,
But soon we're sure we shall hear more of them!

"Awful," Betsy grumbled in a low whisper.
They hid behind the hanging curtains against the back

wall as the Midions trooped out, all except Augustus seeming very pleased with themselves. "You were in excellent voice, Mrs. Midion," Junius said heartily. "I am sure you will make a most popular hit."

"Thank you, Mr. Midion," returned his wife. "I am only sorry about poor Katrina Three."

"Well, they do wear out, you know," Junius said. "She shall be put to ushering until she falls apart, and tomorrow morning, as I shall be performing a few little spells anyway, I shall conjure Katrina Four. Fortunately, her part in the play is so very small that I think the new one shall do quite well with a minimum of rehearsal." His voice faded off down the corridor.

Jarvey and Betsy waited for several minutes. The Midions seemed to have departed, and the stage lay empty before they dared to move. "Who's Katrina Three?" Betsy asked.

Jarvey's damp clothes clung to him and chilled him, so his teeth were almost chattering as he answered: "One of the magical actresses, I think," Jarvey said. "They seem a little bit realer than the audience, but I don't think they're permanent. I suppose if they get out of whack, Junius just junks them and then makes new ones to replace them. Let's get out of the auditorium where we can see what we're doing, and we'll try the Grimoire."

They stepped out onto the stage, now only dimly lighted, went around the sailing-ship set, and headed for the orchestra pit.

But before they had taken more than a few steps, something white swooped down on them from the wings. "I've caught you!" shrieked a horrible, scratchy voice. "Help! Help!"

A bony hand closed on Jarvey's arm, and the creature that had pounced from the gloom grabbed Betsy with the other hand. Their captor was a woman, or what was left of one.

Jarvey could hardly recognize the decaying ruin as one of the younger actresses he had seen in the dressing room. Her skin had become cracked and peeling, and her eyelids had withered away, leaving her bloodshot eyeballs staring madly out of their sockets. Cracked and flaking skin barely covered her skull, and what skin remained had become rough and dry-looking, like old, rotting leather. Her auburn hair was falling off in big clumps, and her blackened lips had pulled away from her gums, leaving her mouth a gaping slash in her face. Many of her teeth had fallen out, giving her a horrible jagged grin, and the arms that had reached to seize Jarvey and Betsy had great pits in the flesh.

Betsy screamed in terror as this corpse-like creature began to drag them back, her grip surprisingly strong. "Master!" the monstrous woman shrieked. "Master! See what I have! Let me live! Master!"

Jarvey struggled to free himself, swatted at her hand, and felt cold, rigid flesh strung with cord-like muscle and tendons. She gripped him even tighter, her hand like a trap snapped closed on his flesh. With a lurching gait, she dragged the two of them into the darkness of the wings.

"Enough!"

"Massterrr," gargled Katrina Three through her dissolving larynx. "Ssssseeeee."

"Light!"

All the stage lights flared up full. Junius Midion stood leaning on a cane, glowering at them. At his elbow, Augustus leered at them in triumph. "I told you, Father."

"Lett mmmmeee llllivvve," pleaded Katrina Three.

"You remained alone onstage after the curtain fell?" asked Junius, sounding shocked. "You know that will destroy you! I can't save you. However, I give you a quick and painless release." Junius snapped his fingers, and with a gurgle of anguish, the creature holding Jarvey's arm collapsed in on herself, her fingers stretching away to wispy streams, sticky as cobweb before they dissolved.

Betsy, suddenly released from the hold she had been fighting against, fell backward onto the stage, thumping her head hard, and Jarvey staggered. He felt something firm pressing against his chest. Junius was prodding him with his cane. "How did you get here, boy?" he asked.

Jarvey didn't answer.

A moment later, though, Junius's dark blue eyes flew wide as he saw what Jarvey was holding under one arm.

"The Grimoire!" he shouted. "Seize the boy, Augustus. He must not be allowed to live!"

7

The Rest Is Silence

"Don't open the book!" Junius Midion snarled at his son. They stood in the last dressing room, the one the Midion family used. "Augustus, I warn you!"

Augustus had carried the Grimoire into the room and had placed it on the table in front of one of the mirrors. His fingers twitched, and he had reached forward, had actually begun to open it, but when Junius Midion cracked his cane down on the cover with a sharp sound as startling as a gunshot his son had taken a reluctant step back. "Augustus, listen to me. We shall deal with the Grimoire in good time. Go bring the girl."

70

As a disgruntled-looking Augustus turned and left the dressing room, Junius roughly shoved Jarvey backward into a chair. "Now, my fine young fellow, you owe us a considerably detailed explanation. Who are you, and what have you done? Why have you brought the Grimoire here? Don't you realize how very dangerous that is?"

"I know," Jarvey said through clenched teeth. "It can destroy this crazy world you've built."

"Look at me!"

Jarvey found himself unable to resist the stern order. Junius stared into Jarvey's eyes, frowning. "I see. You are actually one of us. You fit the old rhyme so exactly, midnight eyes, hair like rusty gold. What is your name, boy?"

"I'm a Midion," Jarvey said. No use in hiding that.

"Midion is an ancient and fearsome name. How do you come to have the Grimoire?"

"I got it from the man who was writing the latest chapter," Jarvey growled. "I've had it for a long time now."

"Ah. The latest in the line of sorcerers to hold the book, and yet you are so young. What year do you come from, back on the dear departed Earth?"

Jarvey returned his stare with as much defiance as he could muster. "I left Earth about a hundred and seventy years after you did," he said.

"So long after my own time! Dear me. I'm sure the cultured world of your age still remembers the famous Midion Theatrical Family. And tell me now, what world were you building when you blundered into mine? That's quite against our family rules, you know, one sorcerer interfering with another's paradise."

"I wasn't building any old world," Jarvey said. "I was trying to get out, not in."

Junius frowned. "You need not lie to me. A Midion has but one use for the Grimoire, and that is to create the world of his delight. For me and my family, that world is the theater, with all its divine illusion and rewards. For my younger brother, it was to be a world of hunting and stalking. One of my remote ancestors even created a frozen world of human statues, where no one at all lived and moved but he. To each his own, you see. Now, you—"

"Father!"

Junius whirled on his heel as Augustus appeared in the doorway. "What's happened now?"

"She's gone."

"What? Impossible. She was unconscious . . ." Junius turned back to Jarvey. "Or did she exist at all, I wonder? Was the girl real or a phantasm?"

"I don't know what you mean."

Junius stood back, with one hand almost caressing the cover of the Grimoire, and began to chant something softly. A column of air beside him shimmered, grew misty, and then began to take on the vague outlines of a human shape. At first a milky white skeleton, then a blur of hair, flesh, and clothing, and—Jarvey could not help shivering—a duplicate of the vanished Katrina, but a Katrina undecayed and in the full bloom of youth and beauty, had shimmered into existence.

"Katrina Four," Junius said. "My dear, you are to play the role of lady's maid to the countess. Your first line is in Act Two, Scene One. The cue is 'Pack all my trunks.'"

"Oh, dear, m'um, I shall never be able to survive a long sea voyage," the woman said. "Already I feel the stirring of seasickness."

"Phantasms are very practical as secondary characters, you see," Junius remarked with a smirk. "None of that tedious memorizing of lines needed. Katrina, my dear, somewhere in the auditorium is a young woman. Go out and find her and kill her, if you please."

Katrina curtsied and glided toward the door.

"No! Don't!" Jarvey yelled, leaping up.

The hard tip of Junius's cane caught him in the chest and pushed him down into his chair again. "So your friend is not a phantasm, then, but real. Very good. Katrina, forget what I told you. Go find her, and when you find her, seize her and call for me. Mind you do not step onto the stage alone! That is fatal."

"Yes, Mr. Midion."

"Augustus, take our kinsman to our rooms and let your mother and sister know he is quite dangerous. He is not to be trusted, and I want them to keep a close eye on him. I will hold the book here."

"Come on, you," Augustus said, grabbing Jarvey's arm. "Oh, I say! He's all damp and nasty, Father."

"Take him along. He will dry in time."

With the bigger and stronger Augustus behind him, Jarvey found himself stumbling down the hallway that led first to the Midions' apartment, then to the door leading out to the garden. His mind whirled. How could he escape? He couldn't overpower Augustus, and even if he did, he couldn't run this way. They'd trap him for sure in the garden, and hiding out in the apartment was crazy.

"Here," Augustus said, thrusting Jarvey through the apartment door. "Mother! Honoria! Look here. I was right after all!"

"And your father was wrong," Jarvey said.

Augustus thumped him in the back. "Shut it, you."

74

Sarah and Honoria Midion came in, looking shocked. "Oh, my," Sarah said, pacing around Jarvey, but keeping a careful distance. "Is he real?"

Honoria stayed well back and crossed her arms as she made a grimace of disgust. "He looks like a drowned rat," she said with a sniff.

"Sit here, boy, and dry a little." Sarah pointed toward the fireplace, and with a flash and a whumping sound, a crackling fire sprang magically to life. Jarvey huddled in front of it, grateful for the warmth but wondering what had happened to Betsy.

"You were right about what you said to your father in the garden too," Jarvey muttered again to Augustus. "You're all rotten actors."

Honoria's face flushed. "What did you say, you horrid little beast?"

"It's true," Jarvey insisted. "Augustus knows it's true. Nobody liked your old plays, and they thought you were about the worst actors in the world!"

"Child, you are speaking without knowledge," Sarah Midion said, her face pinched with disapproval. She made a grand, sweeping gesture. "We performed in London and Paris! In England, we toured all through the country, and—"

"I know about your performances," Jarvey said. "Augustus does too. He told your husband that his plays were no good, that the people laughed at the tragedies and—"

"What do common people know of art?" Honoria demanded. "Mother, make this dreadful child be still."

"Please do be silent," Sarah said to Jarvey. "Or else I shall have to do things to you that you would not much care for, my dear."

Jarvey shivered at the smooth, calm threat in her tone. Sarah Midion was a Midion only by marriage, and she sounded very soft and motherly, but the look in her eyes was ferocious and deadly. He glanced at Augustus, who stood leaning on the mantel, his face closed and brooding. Jarvey thought that Augustus even looked as if he were onstage, playing the part of an angry young man.

The minutes crawled past. Finally Junius Midion entered the room, the Grimoire in his hands. "Your little friend is quite clever," he growled. "But we are clever here too, as you shall learn. Perhaps she thinks she can hide from me. She is deceived. My boy, you may be a Midion, but your magic is certainly no match for my own."

"Father," said Augustus suddenly, "why can't we use the Grimoire?"

"To do what?" Junius asked. "To find one urchin of a pestilential girl? That would be like using a cannon to kill a mosquito, my boy. No, no, I will simply call up our audience, and they will scour every inch of the theater. She cannot hide forever."

"I didn't mean use the Grimoire to find the girl," Augustus said. "Let's use it to get out of this."

His father stared at him. "To get out of what, Augustus?"

"This world!" Augustus snapped. "You may like performing in play after play forever, but you're the star, you're always the star! And none of it is real, Father! I'm a Midion too. I want a world where I can—"

"Impossible," Junius hissed. "You have no idea what you're asking, Augustus. Do you really want to go back to a world of fools and dunces who don't appreciate you, who have no conception of the noble art of the theater?"

"You never asked me if I wanted to be in the theater in the first place," grumbled Augustus. "Yes, I remember what it was like being cold and hungry because the theater owner closed our show after one performance. I remember traveling through the mud and mire to get from one dirty little town to the next. I even remember what it felt like when the audience pelted us with rotten tomatoes and old cabbages!"

"Augustus!" his mother said.

A wild look had sprung into Junius's eyes. "None of that matters! None of that is real here! This is our world. Augustus, if there is something you do not like, we can change it freely here. There are no fools about to interfere or to stop us. None except this one."

Jarvey swallowed as Junius Midion spun and pointed his finger right into Jarvey's face. The family was ready to go for each other's throats, he realized. Maybe they had been making believe too long, with no one real around them. After nearly two hundred years of the same thing day after day, they just might be tired of each other's company. And if he could goad them, maybe they would turn on each other, not on him. "Augustus knows the truth," he croaked. "This is all just make-believe. None of it is real."

"You're wrong, young Midion," Junius said, his lips nearly white with anger. "My world is very real. As real as life and as real as . . . death." His finger stabbed again.

Jarvey screeched as his stomach felt as though it had exploded into fire. He had never felt such pain. He pitched forward from the chair and slammed into the floor, not even registering the impact. He was like a bug on a hot skillet, fire was consuming him . . .

Then it passed, and he lay gasping on the floor. "Just a small sample of how real pain can be here, in this imaginary world of mine," Junius told him. "We have two problems now. One is your blighted playmate, who got away from my foolish son. The other is the Grimoire. It should not be in this world, but back on Earth. If it were accidentally opened here to the right passage, our whole world would be swept out of existence. However, if we send it back to Earth, even if it should be destroyed on Earth, our world would be safe forever. I think once we find the girl, we can solve both problems at once. I shall send you back to Earth with the Grimoire. But perhaps I shall send you to Earth as it was ten million years ago. That should keep you and the book safe. I do not think you have enough magic in you to overcome so huge a gap in time."

"But he might," said his wife.

"Not," Junius replied with a smile, "if I take away his mouth, his ears, and his eyes before I send him on his last journey. Not then, I fancy."

Jarvey could not sleep that night. The Midions threw him into a small room and tossed in some blankets, but sleep was impossible. He worked at the door, but although it seemed to have no lock at all, Junius had enchanted it

79

and it would not open. It had become only a painted illusion of a door, like part of a stage set, and not a real door at all.

The room gave him nothing to work with, no tools for escape. It was hardly more than a closet, with shelves of shoes and hats lining three of the walls. One of those uncanny candles emitted a little feeble light. Jarvey clenched his hands. If he had his way, he thought, the evil magicians like Junius would all be banished from the pages of the Grimoire. If he ever mastered the art of magic, he could use the book for good, not evil.

He could destroy all the chapters created by the evil magicians of the past. Then he could re-create his own world, and his parents would live there, happy and rich. And he would be the best baseball player in the world, he'd win game after game. And there would be no one, no one at all, with hateful or angry feelings, because if there were, he'd banish them forever.

Jarvey crouched in a corner and lost himself in fantasies of magic and revenge. If only . . .

If only he could get his hands on the Grimoire.

He took a deep breath. Zoroaster had warned him about this. The Grimoire could corrupt a Midion, could make him believe that he was only acting for the best—but the evil book would trap its user in the end. No, there had to be some other way.

Hours passed before the door opened and Augustus kicked his shin. "Come on, you. Father wants you in the theater." The older boy reached in, grabbed his shoulder, and hauled him to his feet.

Jarvey hadn't eaten in a long time, but Augustus let him pause only for a quick drink of water. He felt sweaty and dirty as Augustus prodded him down the hall and into the wings of the theater. Junius stood on a bare stage there, the sailing-ship set gone. The only piece of furniture remaining was a tall kind of desk or book stand, and on top of it lay the closed Grimoire, its reddish-brown cover gleaming dully in the stage lights.

Jarvey heard a muted sound of low voices, and squinting against the light streaming down onto the stage, he saw a shadowy crowd in the seats: the audience. "We shall find her, you know," Junius said casually to Jarvey. "She must be here somewhere. You could save us so much time by calling her to come out from hiding."

Jarvey balled his fists and stared sullenly at the floor.

He heard Junius sigh dramatically. "No? Very well, then, it is up to the patrons of the theater."

He raised his voice: "My friends! We have here in our

midst this young man. He has lost his dear friend, a young lady with red hair, clothed in gray and white. This will be an exciting game of theatrical hide-and-seek! My friends, you are to explore this theater and find that girl and bring her to me now!"

The audience stirred, rising from the seats, trudging through the auditorium. Junius turned to Jarvey. "And if they do not find her in thirty minutes' time," he said softly and almost pleasantly, "I shall begin to maim you, my boy, very slowly, with much pain, here on the stage. Your screams of anguish will bring her out, I believe. Then we shall have our little farewell party for you two."

Some of the milling crowd climbed up onto the edge of the stage, while others roamed the auditorium, looking under seats, going out through the passageways, even scanning the high ceiling. Jarvey shuddered as the mindless things plodded past him, splitting into two streams, one going off into the wings on the left, the other on the right.

Augustus stood behind Jarvey, gripping the back of his shirt. Jarvey stared longingly at the Grimoire. It was just ten or twelve feet away. If he could only reach it . . . but that was hopeless. Junius had not stirred from his place beside the book stand. Even if Jarvey could somehow pull himself free from Augustus's grip, Junius would snatch the book up before Jarvey could take more than a step or two.

Jarvey whispered to Augustus, "I wouldn't let him send the Grimoire away if I were you. That will leave you trapped here in the theater forever."

"Quiet," Augustus grunted, poking him.

Jarvey felt nervous sweat creeping over his face. "I'd go crazy, acting in these stupid plays for all eternity, with nobody real at all."

"Be *quiet*," Augustus warned, giving Jarvey a shake.

Junius heard that, and he turned and took the few steps over to them. "What are you arguing about?"

"I was telling him that if you send the Grimoire away, he'll have to do just what you want him to do forever," Jarvey replied. "I don't think he likes that."

"You *are* a fool," Junius said. "Isn't he, son?"

Augustus didn't reply for a moment. Then he said querulously, "Father, he has a point. This is the world you wanted, not the one I want."

"It is our world, and that's an end," Junius pronounced. "Don't listen to this young troublemaker, son. I don't know how he muddled his way into our world, but he has no real power, of that I'm certain. He can't even defend himself against a simple magical attack—"

Jarvey jerked around, staring toward a dark corner of the wings, and yelled, "No! Leave her alone! Let her go!"

Instantly, Junius turned, raising his arm. Augustus let go his hold on Jarvey's shirt at the same moment, and he and Jarvey leaped forward, both reaching for the Grimoire.

In the second or two that it took Junius to realize that Jarvey had faked him out, the book stand crashed to the stage, and Augustus and Jarvey dived to the floor, wrestling for possession of the Grimoire like two football players falling on a fumbled ball.

"Get out of the way!" shouted Junius, dancing from side to side.

Jarvey kicked and rolled and twisted, trying to wrench the tall, narrow volume from the grip of the older boy. "Let—go!"

"It's mine!" Augustus growled, pummeling Jarvey's shoulder with one hand while he tried to pull the book free with the other.

Just as he lost his grip on the Grimoire, Jarvey saw Junius's lips move, saw his pointing finger, and with all his strength rolled aside as an invisible blast of magic struck Augustus, causing him to scream in pain and drop the Grimoire. Jarvey dived for it, retrieved it like a football player recovering a fumble, and then scrambled to his feet, dreading the spell that would hit him at any moment—

"Here!" Betsy's voice! She had thrown back a trapdoor and stood in the black square. "Look out!"

Too late. Junius's spell made Jarvey's legs go dead under him, and he toppled forward. Betsy grabbed his shoulders as he went sprawling, and she dropped down, hauling him with her. Dimly, Jarvey realized she had been standing almost on the top rung of a tall ladder, but she lost her footing and they both fell. Jarvey clung to the Grimoire as they spun through the air, then gasped as he landed on his back, the breath rushing from his lungs. Betsy had him by the shoulder and was dragging him, and up above he saw a square of light, the opening of the trapdoor in the stage above.

Clutching the Grimore to his chest, Jarvey panted, "Cl-close! Close now! I command it! *Close and be sealed!*"

And something happened, some force rushed out of him. He felt it, and a moment later the trapdoor overhead slammed shut with an echoing crash. He had borrowed enough magic from the Grimoire to do that.

But how could they escape from beneath the stage itself?

His legs tingled with a terrible pins-and-needles feeling, as though he had been badly shocked, but at least some feeling was creeping back. "Come on," Betsy gasped in the dark. "Can't you walk?"

Leaning on her, Jarvey staggered to his feet. He felt as if the floor were heaving and rising and falling like the deck of a ship in a storm, but he lurched along in the dark. Betsy threw open a door . . .

And they burst into one of those endless marble hallways.

A dismal shout rose from a group of the audience members off to their left. Jarvey spun and raced away from them, with Betsy pounding along close beside him. The corridor turned a sharp corner to the right, and as they turned it, Jarvey saw a door opening not far ahead.

His heart sank as Junius Midion stepped through, his face a mask of fury. Jarvey skidded to a stop. "Do it!" Betsy yelled, grabbing his arm. "Do it before he gets his hands on the book!"

"A-abrire," Jarvey shouted, his fingers fumbling at the catch that kept the book closed.

He felt Betsy's grip tighten on his left arm.

Ahead of him, Junius pointed and shouted, *"Frater!"*

As if it heard Junius, the book flew open, an invisible hand reached out, and Jarvey heard Betsy scream in alarm as the book pulled them inside.

8

Sea Change

Darkness roared in Jarvey's ears like a strong wind. For a moment he didn't know where or even who he was.

He forced himself to open his eyes, dreading what he might see. At first everything drifted in his sight in a shifting gray, foggy blur: dim moving figures and floating patches of light, pale in the darkness. Then, almost as if by magic, his mother's face materialized from the fog, close by, so close he could reach up and touch her if he had the strength. "Jarvey?" she asked softly. "Are you all right? How do you feel?"

His father's bespectacled face loomed over her right shoulder. "How many fingers am I holding up?"

Jarvey had to close his right eye to focus on his father's hand. "T-two," he said. "What happened? Where am I?"

His mom and dad hugged each other for a moment, and then in a strangely husky voice, his dad said, "You're in the hospital, son. You got hurt a little. Do you remember what happened in the baseball game?"

Jarvey tried to shake his head and discovered he was rolling it back and forth on a soft pillow instead. And it hurt to do even that much. His forehead throbbed with waves of dull pain, making him wince and making his eyes water. A blood-pressure cuff was clamped around his right biceps, feeling far too tight. He croaked, "I don't remember any game. What happened?" The weak sound of his own voice shocked him. He sounded exhausted and feeble, even to himself.

"You got smacked hard by a line drive," a third voice said. The voice sounded deep and hearty, a man's voice, but it was one he didn't recognize. Through the lingering gray fog, Jarvey could make out a white-coated figure standing at the foot of the bed. The drifting dimness concealed the man's face. "Jarvis, you have a condition that we doctors call 'traumatic amnesia.' That means your brain got a little scrambled by a hard blow, so you probably can't remember anything that happened to you during the game."

"I don't," Jarvey said, squinting, trying to make out the doctor's face.

"Not unusual. Now, while you were unconscious, you may have had some pretty vivid dreams. Don't let them bother you. Your x-rays look fine. How do you feel?"

Jarvey felt incredibly achy. His muscles and joints hurt in a hundred different places. In fact, he felt less as though he'd been hit on the head than as if he'd tripped and fallen down a whole flight of stairs. "I hurt," he said. "And I'm a little hungry."

The doctor lifted his arm and glanced down at his watch. "Your nurse will be around shortly. Let her know if you'd like anything special for tea. Mr. and Mrs. Midion, Jarvey will be fine now. What he needs most is just plain ordinary bed rest, so say good bye to him for a little while and we'll let him watch the telly or whatever he feels like doing."

Jarvey's mom gave him a gingerly hug and a peck on the cheek, and his dad gave him a grin and a wave. Then the adults left, sort of vanishing into the fog, and he lay frowning.

The nurse would come in soon to ask what he wanted . . . for *tea?*

The doctor had said "tea" as if it were a meal, and he had spoken of the "telly." Those were British words, Jarvey thought, not American. "No," he groaned. "Not again."

He reached to rip off the irritatingly tight blood-pressure cuff. It moved before he could touch it, feeling not like Velcro at all, but like something alive. It let go of his arm but grabbed his hand with strong fingers.

Jarvey yelped and tried to pull away, fighting the ghostly grip. The door banged open, and the doctor rushed in, brandishing a hypodermic needle that looked as though it were made for an elephant, a huge thing six inches long.

And the doctor's writhing, triumphant face was the furious face of the spidery man who had crept over the chain-link fence in Jarvey's nightmare.

"Now I have you!" shrieked the man, raising the needle high, ready to plunge it down.

"Jarvey, wake up!"

Betsy's voice, soft but urgent in his ear.

Jarvey tried to roll aside, toppled out of the bed, and felt himself falling. "It was a dream," he gasped in midair.

A moment later Jarvey landed hard, with a crash that made yellow light flare behind his eyes. His chest heaved, trying to draw breath into his empty lungs. For a few moments he couldn't remember clearly what had just happened, let alone take stock of where he was. The hard, hot surface below him seemed to heave and roll. When he forced his eyes open, he found he was staring straight up, but all he could see was a kind of billowing white emptiness.

"Are you all right?"

Betsy's voice, from somewhere close by. Fighting panic, Jarvey whispered, "I think I'm blind."

Something more or less pink waved in front of his face, and he focused on Betsy's hand. "See that?"

With a groan, Jarvey pushed himself up. "I was dreaming. I thought . . . Where are we?"

Beneath her coppery hair, her face was bunched up in an expression of concern. "On a boat. At sea."

One thing from his dream carried over into reality: the pain. Jarvey felt as if he had been struck by a car. His whole body ached miserably. At least he was breathing normally again. Now he saw that he lay far forward on the deck of a sailing ship, and the white, billowy nothingness he had been staring up toward was actually a huge rectangular sail. Beyond and above it was a blue sky filled with puffy white clouds. A bewilderment of ropes led up to the mast, and on the high yardarms crept men, their forms made tiny by distance, who were hauling on the sail. No one seemed to notice that two stowaways had just come aboard. Jarvey clutched his aching ribs and then looked around the empty deck in sudden panic. "Where's the Grimoire?"

"I don't know. Didn't you hold on to it?"

"I had it until we hit! Look for it!" Jarvey rolled to his stomach and pushed himself up to a kneeling position. His head reeled, partly from the shock of passage from Junius Midion's world to this one, partly from the vessel's movement. He and Betsy had almost missed the deck entirely. They had landed in the small triangular area at the very front of the ship, partly underneath the boom that stuck out forward and supported the jib sails. Coils of rope hung from cleats, and small chests cluttered the deck, each of them lashed down to ring bolts set in the wood. The Grimoire might have slipped behind one—if it hadn't fallen into the water!

Jarvey hauled himself to his feet and looked wildly around. Gray ocean spread out on all sides, its restless surface streaked with white foam and crawling with waves. Now he could smell the salty ocean air, mixed with tar and the scent of sun-heated wood. Betsy went from one chest to the other, bending and peering. "I don't see it!"

"Has to be here somewhere," Jarvey said, taking a staggering step to help her look.

But Betsy turned and tugged his arm. "Someone's coming! Follow me."

She slipped over the rail. Jarvey heard voices approaching, and he quickly scrambled up and over, dropping down onto a kind of platform attached to the bows. Ropes from it stretched tautly up toward the forward mast, and behind these ropes crouched Betsy. She held a finger to her lips.

Jarvey's head spun a little. They sat on a plank a little more than a foot wide, their legs dangling, their hands clutching the thick ropes, and beneath their feet the ocean rose and fell, rose and fell, as the ship's bow rode a wave or plunged down into a trough, sending a foamy spray of salt water flying. Jarvey fought back nausea. He was getting seasick.

Just behind him, on the deck, a man was speaking. "Unload these last. They are not important to the Nawab, but they should bring us a pretty profit."

"Aye, sir. 'Twill take most of tomorrow to empty the holds. Save these for the day after, then?"

"Yes. And after the crew has finished unloading them,

let the men know they may have the next three nights ashore before we sail again."

"Aye, sir."

The voices rumbled off into the distance. "Where do you think we are?" Betsy asked.

Jarvey stared at her. "How should I know?"

"You opened the book!"

"Yes, but Junius Midion yelled something just as I did. '*Frater.*' What does that mean?"

Betsy shook her head. "Dunno. Maybe the name of this ship?"

"Could be. We've got to find the Grimoire. Think it's safe to climb back over now?"

"Let me go look. You're green in the face."

Jarvey's pride was hurt, but in fact he felt happy just to cling to his ropes and rest there. How long had it been since he had eaten? He couldn't remember, but at the moment he felt that he would throw up everything he had ever swallowed in his life if he moved at all. Betsy took a cautious look over the rail, then slipped over as quietly as a sea breeze.

Jarvey tried focusing his gaze ahead on the horizon, hoping that would keep his stomach from lurching so much. He sat in the shade of the ship now, with the sun low in the sky over to his left. The day had the hot feel of afternoon about it, so with sunset to his left, Jarvey guessed they were sailing north.

A cottony pile of clouds had built up dead ahead, purple on their shadowed side, pink and white on the sunward one. Squinting, Jarvey could just make out a dark gray smudge of land at their base.

A moment later, a triumphant Betsy swung back over, clutching something under her left arm. "Got it! It was behind the box right in the front, wedged tight. Here." She grimaced as she passed the volume over.

"Thanks." Jarvey took the narrow book in both hands. "Should I open it?"

Betsy squirmed. "Dunno. What if your mother and father are here? Best to wait, maybe, until we know where we are. I'd say hold on a bit. Keep it safe."

Safe! What if Jarvey dropped the book now, a few feet above the ocean? Carefully he tucked it into his shirt. He had become so used to carrying the thing that it felt almost like a part of him. "Well, anyway, we can't sit out here all night," he said to Betsy. "What are we going to do?"

"Rest a while and wait until dark," she replied. "Won't be long."

But it felt like hours and hours as the ship responded to

the winds, the men trimming the sails sometimes within earshot but most of the time not. At last the light faded, the sky darkened and stars came out, and Betsy said, "Let's go. Hold on to the book."

She was as sure-footed as a cat, and about as silent. They climbed over the rail, and she led the way through the darkness back toward the stern of the ship. Two men stood at the wheel, just behind the middle mast, talking about the weather. In the darkness a crouching Jarvey and Betsy slipped past without their noticing.

At the stern rail, Betsy whispered, "Thought so. Here's where we stay tonight."

A wooden lifeboat or longboat or something hung from two tall metal hooks. Betsy worked at the cords holding a canvas cover over the boat, tight as the head of a drum, until it grew loose enough for them to squirm underneath it and drop into the boat. The air trapped under the canvas felt humid and hot, stiflingly so, and Jarvey gasped as he crawled into the swinging boat. "Now what?" he asked. It was as dark as the bottom of a coal mine.

"Boats like this generally have food and water stored in case the ship sinks," she whispered. "Can you give us some light?"

"How?" he asked sarcastically.

"You're the magician."

Jarvey clenched his jaw. No, as he had tried and tried to explain to Betsy, he wasn't a magician, not really. Tantalus Midion, the evil master of Lunnon, had taunted him about that. True, people in his family were sometimes born with a talent for magic, just as they tended to be born with dark blue eyes and blond hair streaked with reddish tones. The magic missed some of them, though. Jarvey's dad was as ordinary as a warm day in June, and though Betsy was a remote cousin of his, she couldn't do magic either.

And while it was true that magical things sometimes happened around Jarvey, he had no idea how to control them. But Betsy kept insisting that he should be able to perform magic. He growled, "Abracadabra, I want light. See? Nothing happened."

Betsy grumbled, "You're not even trying." Jarvey felt her fumbling with something and then she found his hand and thrust something into his grip. "Here, make one of those strange candles, like the ones in old Junius's theater."

"What is this?" It felt like a short round piece of wood, not like wax.

"Dunno. It's a wooden peg or something, felt it rolling around loose on the bottom of this boat. Turn it into a candle."

"I don't know how!"

Betsy was nothing if not stubborn, sometimes annoyingly so. "Try! You made that trapdoor slam shut! And you could make people not notice you back in Lunnon, when they were hunting you! Remember how those strange candles looked and felt. Then command that piece of wood to be just the same. Picture it. Imagine it."

"I might as well imagine a turkey dinner and a hot bath," grumbled Jarvey. He tried, though. Holding the wooden peg, he visualized in his mind the candle he had taken from the sconce back in the theater. The candle had been lighter in weight, and the surface felt smooth and cool, not rough and splintery. The flame was a teardrop of cool yellow light. He tried to persuade himself that he was holding the candle at that moment.

"You got to say something, I think," Betsy whispered.

Jarvey took a deep breath, held it, and then said, "Let this be a candle."

He felt something, a twitch of power, or maybe the ship had just changed course. But the darkness didn't lift.

"You want light," Betsy said. "Not just a candle, but a lighted candle. Try that."

Jarvey squeezed the thing he was holding. Did it feel somehow waxier, more like a candle than wood, or was he just fooling himself? He couldn't tell. "Let this candle give us light," he said.

Nothing.

He heard Betsy sigh.

Unreasonable anger filled Jarvey, partly because he still ached, partly because he took Betsy's sigh as a sarcastic hint that she didn't think much of him. "Light!" he snarled, so loudly that Betsy shushed him.

But something happened at last. Jarvey blinked. The candle was giving a kind of glow. It was so dim that the difference between darkness and its light was hardly any difference at all, but at one end of the thing he held, a spherical red spark shone. He could barely make out Betsy's face.

"You did it!" she said, her eyes wide.

Still feeling grumpy, he whispered, "I'm the magician, remember?"

The candle obstinately refused to burn any brighter, but gradually their eyes adjusted to the feeble gleam. Betsy found a row of wooden kegs tucked under the forward seat of the lifeboat. A tin cup was tied to one of the kegs, and she undid the cord. Then she pulled a cork that plugged the nearest keg and held the cup beneath the gush of water that poured out. It was very warm and tasted of wood, but they drank it anyway. After pounding the cork back into place, Betsy squirmed toward the stern and after a few minutes came back with a bulky package wrapped in what felt like thick canvas soaked in wax. "Ship's biscuit," she said, peeling the canvas away. "Here."

The flat thing she handed him was nearly as hard as a rock, but Jarvey crunched it and immediately felt his hunger rise. They found that by dribbling a little water on the biscuit, they could soften it enough to chew and swallow.

"Best get some sleep if we can," Betsy said at last, and she crept back toward the rear of the boat. "Put out the light."

"Easy for you to say." Jarvey couldn't blow out the flame, because the candle had no flame, just a little round red glow about the size of a marble. It didn't even feel hot. Finally he pulled the cork from the water keg, stuck the candle into the hole, light first, and shut off the glow that way.

Then Jarvey stretched out as well as he could, tried to ignore the constant movement, the pitching and rolling, and the sick feeling that he was lost.

Best get some sleep, Betsy had said.

Jarvey wasn't sure he wanted to try.

Because when he slept, he was likely to dream.

9

Unsafe Harbor

*B*etsy nudged him awake. "C'mon. Almost daylight. Quiet, now!"

Feeling giddy with weariness, Jarvey checked to make sure the Grimoire was still safely buttoned inside his shirt, then followed her out, worming his way under the tight canvas cover and dropping down to the deck. It was still dark, though a lot cooler than it had been. He frowned. The ship's motion felt very different, much steadier. As soon as his feet touched the deck, Betsy pulled him back into the shadowed darkness under the hanging lifeboat. Ahead, reddish-orange torches flared, and in their ruddy light, Jarvey could see that the ship had glided to a pier. Figures were busy with mooring ropes, snugging the ship up against wooden pilings. No one glanced back toward them.

"We can climb over the rail and jump to the dock," Betsy whispered. "Be quick and be quiet, though."

"Okay."

He followed her, but when he poised himself on the rail of the ship, he almost turned back. Because of the curve of the deck, the rail was a good five feet from the edge of the dock, and the dock lay in almost total darkness. If he misjudged the leap, he would drop straight into the water—

"Hey! Away from there, you thievin' brat!"

Someone was rushing toward him. Jarvey didn't hesitate, but jumped out into space as hard and as far as he could. He hit the pier and sprawled flat, then scrambled to his feet and clutched at the Grimoire, still safe inside his shirt. Betsy was running away already, and he stumbled after her, hearing the man up on the ship's deck curse him and bark out, "Keep an eye out for wharf rats, men! These beggar children will get aboard and steal us blind."

One of the crew, already standing on the pier, lashed out with the end of a rope as Jarvey raced past. The man missed, but Jarvey heard the rope hiss through the dark air and even felt the breeze of it on his cheek. He caught up with Betsy a second later. They passed the prow of the ship, and then pelted down the long pier and onto a cobbled street. There Betsy stopped short, gasping for air, and Jarvey blundered right into her. "What now?"

"Get our bearin's," she said. "Get some food. Get some clothes." She sniffed. "Get a bath, if we can. You need one."

"So do you," he growled.

They were in a town of low one-story buildings, hushed and quiet in the hour before sunrise. Betsy's keen nose led them to a place where someone was cooking something. Jarvey's mouth started to water at a scent like bananas and fresh-baked bread. It seemed to be a simple kind of restaurant, with a long counter along the front and a few people inside bending over stoves and opening ovens. They walked past it, and then Betsy said, "Wait," and slipped away. Jarvey stood in a darkened doorway as she melted off into the twilight.

The sky had begun to show streaks of dawn by the time she returned a few minutes later. "Here," she said, thrusting something warm into his hand. "Eat this."

"What is it?"

"Dunno, but it's loads better than ship's biscuit!"

Jarvey bit into it. It was a sweet banana bread, still warm from the oven, and he ate it voraciously. "Where'd you get it?"

"Slenked it from a little shop," Betsy said shortly. "They've got shelves full of it, never miss a couple of pieces. C'mon, we'll find a place to hole up until we can tell where we are and whether your parents are here."

That was something else Betsy was good at, finding hideouts. Back in Lunnon she and her gang had existed like rats, finding a way to live right under the feet of the masters of the place, and they had never been caught. By the time the sun was well up and people were stirring, Betsy had found a possible hiding place. It was just a neglected and dusty ten-by-ten-foot structure of splintered gray wood, some kind of abandoned storage building, standing right up against a fence. The door creaked open and they slipped inside.

Jarvey's nose twitched. They had disturbed years of dust. No one had used this hut for anything for ages. Three empty wooden crates had been tossed in carelessly, but even they wore a fuzzy coat of ancient dust. Betsy tugged one of these into place so it blocked the door. "How will we get out?" Jarvey asked.

"This way." Betsy tugged and pried at the rotten boards in the back, breaking them off until she had made an escape hatch big enough for them to scramble through on all fours. The fence was right up against the back of the hut, and Jarvey pointed that out. "We can't squeeze into there. I doubt a mouse could do it."

"We're not getting between the house and the fence. We're going *through* the fence," Betsy retorted. Then she kicked at one of the fence boards until it creaked loose at the bottom. Finally she pushed the board aside and took a quick look.

"Lovely. Just a narrow, dark alley behind here, so we can get in and out without having to sneak by a watchman or anything. We're set. Now all we have to do is find out where we are, and what the rules are." She thought for a moment and then said, "Maybe we'd better hide the Grimoire. If we get caught with it . . ."

Uneasily, Jarvey slipped the book from inside his shirt. "You're right. If Siyamon is here, he'll take the book and destroy us. But if we're caught without it, what will we do?"

With a grin, Betsy said, "One of us'll get loose, is what, and come back and get it, and then find some way to free the other. Better to leave it hid. If we're caught, it gives us something to bargain with.

"I guess," Jarvey said. "Where would be a safe place?"

Betsy looked up at the rafters. "Up there," she said. "Can you reach that high?"

He couldn't, but Betsy dragged one of the wooden crates over for him to stand on, and with its added height, Jarvey just managed to slide the Grimoire on top of the middle rafter. You couldn't even see it from floor level. He jumped down. "Will that do?"

"Perfect," she said, dusting her hands. "Now let's go hunting."

Before noon had come, they had found out several things. The town they were in was called Port Midion. The people looked vaguely Indian, with dark complexions and odd clothing, though they sounded completely British. Animals walked freely in the streets: An odd-looking cow with a hump on its back passed them by, and a troupe of monkeys playing some kind of chase game tumbled screeching across the rooftops overhead. They passed some prosperous-looking houses, and Betsy deftly found them new outfits, taken one piece at a time from clotheslines. Before long, both of them wore the local costume, loose-fitting white slipover shirts and trousers.

Best of all, they wandered to a spot with jetting fountains where a host of kids their age and younger splashed and played, and they waded in. It was the first bath Jarvey had ever taken with all his clothes on, but it felt wonderful anyway. Betsy chatted with the kids. Jarvey admired her knack of sounding right at home and cheerful, no matter where she was. Later, after they had left the fountains behind and had walked through the sunny streets until they were reasonably dry again, she said to Jarvey, "Can't quite make out what's what. This isn't as bad as Lunnon, that's plain. Somebody calls himself the Nawab is the lord and master here, but they don't seem to be all that afraid of him. Guess he's a relative of yours."

Jarvey frowned. "I didn't ask to be born a Midion."

"I know. Come on, don't be like that. After all, we're cousins, you know. My grandfather's a Midion." Betsy jerked her head back toward the fountains. "Kids back there didn't know anything about new people in town, but then, they don't know much of anything about the Nawab's doin's, nor even his right name. We'll have to sneak about a little, I think, and keep our ears open. See if this Nawab is your Siyamon Midion or not."

"Do you think he is?"

Betsy sighed, sounding a little irritable. "How should I know? If your Siyamon is like the other Midions, he was writing himself a nice little chapter, wasn't he? Could be he wants to be the ruler of this kind of world. Could be someone else. All I know is that if he's here, your mum and dad are probably not too far away."

"I don't think he could be," Jarvey said slowly. "This place doesn't feel like something from my time."

Betsy shrugged. "Crazy magician can make it feel like anything he wants," she said. "I wish—"

A blare of trumpets cut her off. They had emerged from an alley back onto what seemed to be the main street of the town, a broad cobbled thoroughfare lined with shops. People rushed to get out of the way as a dozen huge men came lurching down the street, preceded by two who sounded trumpets.

Except when they came closer, Jarvey saw they weren't men at all.

"Blimey!" Betsy said.

The creatures that passed by all wore armor and carried spears. But they weren't human.

They were gorillas, walking stooped but on two legs, their heavy heads swinging from side to side and their deep-set brown eyes glaring at the crowd as they passed. As soon as they had gone by, the people seemed to let out a collective sigh of relief, and they went back to their business.

"What was that all about?" Jarvey asked.

"Dunno," Betsy said. "Maybe the Midion that runs this place don't trust men to be his bodyguards. What were those things?"

"Apes," Jarvey said. "Gorillas."

She stared at him, and he realized that on Lunnon there had been no apes. Lunnon had few animals other than cows, pigs, sheep, horses, and dogs. He said, "On Earth, they're creatures from the jungles of Africa. They're stronger than humans, but they're just animals. I mean, they don't dress up in armor and carry weapons. They don't have a language and they can't learn to talk."

"Do they play horns?"

"Huh? Oh, the bugles. No, not the ones on Earth," he said.

They had been walking up a long, gentle slope leading away from the docks, and now they came to a wide market square. Booths all around the edges of it offered everything from fruits and vegetables to carved decorations and clothing. At the center of the square a sort of bulletin board, protected by an overhanging roof, had been built, and men and women paused to read the posters tacked up on it. Jarvey and Betsy paused before this and Jarvey looked at what seemed to be the most recent poster:

A Hunt Is Announced

To-Morrow, for a Period of Three Days
The Nawab Goes Forth to Hunt
You Have Been Warned

"I don't like the sound of that," Jarvey said. "'You have been warned.' What does he do, hunt with cannons or something?"

"We'll have to be careful, looks like," agreed Betsy.

The rest of the day went reasonably well. They got some sense of the world: Midion seemed to be the one important city, but the ships went to and from other settlements, exchanging goods and bringing supplies and luxuries into port. The people in town seemed friendly enough, though wrapped up in their own concerns and not particularly outgoing. Now dressed just like the local inhabitants, Jarvey and Betsy fit in well enough. They wore not only the loose tunics and trousers, but also comfortable sandals, thanks to Betsy's talent at slipping things away while shopkeepers were not looking. No one gave them a second glance.

Betsy was not shy about striking up conversations with strangers, and once when she was talking to a boy who was maybe seven or eight years old, she asked, "So who's the Nawab, then?"

The kid had given her a quizzical glance, his head tilted on one side. "Who's the Nawab? What d'you mean?"

"What's his name?" she asked.

The boy shrugged. "The Nawab, is all. Lives in the palace, owns everything. That's all."

"Where's the palace, then?"

With a snort of laughter, the boy said, "You don't know much, do you? 'S on the hilltop, 'course!"

And that was a help, because the streets of Midion were all very level, all except one. The main street sloped up from the waterfront right through the center of town. They followed it until it ended at the entrance to a green park. A wrought-iron fence taller than Jarvey surrounded the park, and over the tops of the trees three golden onion-domed towers were visible. "That must be the place," Jarvey said. "The palace, where the Nawab lives."

"But we're not going in there," Betsy told him.

He looked ahead. The street ended at the open park gate, but a grassy lane led forward through an avenue of trees and climbed a hill. Jarvey couldn't see anyone walking around in the park at all, but that had to be the way to the palace. "Why not?"

"'Cause look."

Jarvey followed her pointing finger and felt a little sick at what he saw. He had not noticed them before because they blended in so well with the yellow and green grass beside the lane, but now he spotted them. They lay very quietly, very still. You might have mistaken them for a couple of tree branches that had fallen to the ground and that had been carelessly tossed off the pathway.

But they weren't branches. They were snakes, two of them, at least eight feet long each, a mottled greenish-gray. As Jarvey stared at them, they reared, both at once, and spread out their hoods.

Jarvey's heart thumped like a drum. Twenty feet away from him two deadly cobras, their bodies nearly as thick as one of his legs, stared right into his eyes.

"Let's go," Betsy said, tugging at the tail of his tunic.

Jarvey backed away, unwilling to let the deadly creatures out of his sight. They swayed, their heads three feet off the ground, as they watched the two retreat. Finally, when they had gone a good distance, Jarvey forced himself to look ahead, not back at the serpents. "Nice watchdogs," he said.

"And what were they?"

Jarvey explained about cobras. He finished up, "They're about the deadliest snake in the world. If they bite you, you're a goner."

Betsy was frowning. "I didn't know what to call them, but I knew they were evil. Looked like dragons, sort of, in the old stories they tell in Lunnon. Can they be tamed?"

Jarvey shook his head. "I don't think so. But then, gorillas can't be tamed either. These must be—I don't know, magicked or something."

Betsy shivered. "I don't like those things. I'll feel better when we're farther away."

"So will I."

They managed to find another meal. At least, Jarvey thought, this world was richer in its rewards than Junius's theater. The food here was cooked, hot and savory, and satisfyingly filling. Betsy took two shallow wooden bowls from one shop, then in another managed to find them some kind of rice and chicken dish, and finally some bread. They got back to the hut, sneaked in, and talked about what they should do as they ate.

"I think we ought to get a look at this Nawab if we can," Betsy said. "If it's not your Siyamon, we can get out of here and try somewhere else."

"I don't know. Maybe we can find out whether the Nawab is always here or if he comes and goes a lot."

"What good would that do?" Betsy asked, munching some bread.

Jarvey frowned in concentration. "I was in his house back on Earth. It looked like he had tons of stuff there that he'd want to bring with him wherever he ended up. If he's the Nawab, he's probably still spending a good part of his time on Earth."

Betsy was cleaning out her wooden bowl by swabbing a piece of bread over it. She popped the bread into her mouth and said, "That could be the reason the people here don't seem terrified so much as they were in Lunnon. Maybe the Nawab's just a part-time tyrant, like."

Jarvey thought for a long moment. "Maybe. I just wish I could open up the Grimoire and read the last chapter. Then I'd know one way or the other. But every time I open it—"

"You get pulled into another world," Betsy said, setting her bowl down on the crate they had used as a table.

Jarvey nodded. "Yeah. It's like the book hates me and forces me off the track. I don't know what to do about it."

"Zoroaster told you you'd have to learn to use it for one purpose only. To save your parents."

114

"But I can't learn," Jarvey said miserably. "I can't practice, because it yanks me off into some other chapter every time I try to open it. And I don't *know* any magic. The thing is hundreds of years old. It was made by dozens of evil magicians. It's stronger than I am."

"You didn't think you could make a candle either," Betsy pointed out.

Jarvey bit back the words that nearly rushed out. He almost told her that what gave him the ability to create the candle was not magic, but anger and humiliation. He wondered if all the Midion wizards felt the same. Junius Midion, from what he had heard, was furious because the world didn't think he was a very good actor or playwright, and so out of his anger, he created his own warped world, where he was everything he dreamed of being, at least to the ghostly, sad throng of imaginary people who made up his audience. Old Tantalus Midion wanted to be obeyed and feared. He hated people, and from his hatred he made Lunnon, a warped reflection of the London of his own century.

Did hatred and anger hold the key to the book's magic, then? If he simply became desperate enough, mad enough, would he be able to use the Grimoire?

He remembered Zoroaster's refusal to touch the book.

"It would corrupt and ruin me," Zoroaster had said. The Grimoire was just a book, but it was a book that had a kind of spirit of its own. Like a living thing, it fought back and tried to change the person using it. Even someone who was basically good, Zoroaster had warned, could fall prey to the Grimoire's temptations.

Still, if you used it to free people, not to enslave them, if you used it to help your parents and yourself . . . Jarvey sighed. "Let's try to find out just who the Nawab is," he said at last. "If it's Siyamon, we stay. If it isn't, we try the book again."

"Right," Betsy said. She stretched. "Tell me some more about that game you played on Earth. Bias ball?"

Despite everything, Jarvey chuckled. "Baseball," he said. "It's kind of like cricket. But not really." He had read a little about cricket on his first and only day in London, and what he had read made absolutely no sense. "Okay, there are nine on a team in baseball. It's played on a field shaped like a diamond . . ." He talked on and on, sketching out a baseball diamond in the dust atop one of the crates, standing to show Betsy how a pitcher wound up and threw the ball and how a batter got into the proper stance to swing at it.

He finally stopped when she began to yawn hugely. He

settled down to sleep feeling a confusion of emotions. He had been almost happy while talking to Betsy. Baseball was one thing he was good at, that he knew top to bottom. Just for the time of their conversation, Jarvey had almost forgotten about all his troubles while talking about the game he loved. Now, however, knowing just how far away from the game he was, how unlikely it was that he would ever play again, he fought a rising tide of despair.

At least his dreams that night all involved pitching and batting. They woke up at first light, and Betsy said, "Today we find out for sure, right? Today we hit a run home!"

Jarvey knew she was just trying to cheer him up, but he could only muster a weak smile. Then Betsy pushed the fence board aside and they crawled out into the alley.

But when they reached the mouth of the alley, he forgot all about the plan.

That's when he saw the cobras rear up.

The snakes had surrounded them.

10

Where Everything Lives

"Jarvey!" Betsy's voice shook from fear and tension. Jarvey couldn't reply. The snakes had them penned in against the fence. Two gray-green cobras, their hoods spread and their yellow evil eyes sharp, had closed in behind them, and the other six arranged themselves in a deadly ring. All of them were huge, eight or ten feet from nose to tail, and all reared their hooded heads up three feet or more above the ground. Jarvey could hear them hissing, could see their black forked tongues flicking in and out of their fanged mouths, could even smell the musty, sour scent of them.

"Stay still," Jarvey said, his throat feeling scratchy and tight. "Maybe they won't strike if—"

He broke off. Two of the snakes, the two toward the street, were backing away, swaying as they did so. Their heads jerked strangely, almost as if they were gesturing for Jarvey and Betsy to come after them. The ones behind Jarvey and Betsy darted forward. Betsy said, "I—I think they want us to follow them."

"No," Jarvey said. "They're driving us. Don't get too close to them. They aren't friendly." He and Betsy took a couple of steps forward, and the ring of snakes slithered to move along with them, the advance ones backing away, the ones at the side and to the rear following their every movement. People were out, but the moment the snakes and the two young people moved out of the alley and into the street, everyone just melted away, back into the shops and buildings. No one yelled or seemed surprised. They all simply turned away, averting their gazes, and slipped out of sight. Jarvey had the creepy feeling that the people had seen this kind of thing happen before, and that they knew where the cobras were taking them.

Once in the street, six of the cobras spread out behind Jarvey and Betsy. The two "leaders" turned and slithered forward, up the cobbled hill, toward the park. "What are they doing?" Betsy asked.

"I don't know. Maybe they're under the control of the Nawab. We're going toward his palace, anyway."

Jarvey couldn't get over how quickly everyone had fled the streets. The place was like a ghost town, as if word of the snakes had raced ahead. They reached the park gates, and the line of snakes behind them drove them inside. When they came to a fork in the grassy lane, the cobras forced them to the left, away from the onion-domed towers of the palace.

They didn't go far. A tall wall, looking like stucco, sealed off one side of the park. The lane led to an iron-barred wooden gate. One of the gorillas in armor stood beside the wall, head lowered, glowering at them. As they approached, the creature pushed the gate open and gestured toward it. "What are you doing?" Jarvey asked, thinking that maybe, just maybe, animals could talk here.

The ape stared at him with its brown eyes, but it said nothing. "Come on," Betsy said. "Maybe we can get away from the cobras."

Before Jarvey could yell a warning, she broke into a run and hurtled through the open gate. The snakes didn't seem to mind, and the gorilla simply watched her pass by. So Jarvey ran too, rushing through the opening. Behind him, the gorilla slammed the gate with a hollow boom.

"Come on," Betsy said from up ahead. On that side

of the wall the lane had become a narrow, winding path leading into a dense tropical forest. Trees reared up to the sky, their limbs overhung with vines. Birds screeched and chattered, and the air zinged with a million insect sounds.

Jarvey looked back. The gate was still closed. Probably barred too, he thought. He said, "They threw us out of town!"

"Maybe they knew we don't belong here," Betsy said. "Come on. There's bound to be a way back in."

"Back *in*?" Jarvey demanded. "Are you crazy? The snakes are behind that wall!"

"And the Grimoire's back in the hideout," Betsy said.

Jarvey groaned. He'd been so frightened by the deadly snakes that for a moment he'd forgotten the book. "You're right. What do you think we should do?"

"Get in, get the book, and hop onto a ship and hide," Betsy said promptly. "Or else try to use the Grimoire again."

"Okay, how do we get back inside?"

"We'll simply have to find the end of the wall," Betsy said.

Easier said than done. They couldn't always stay within sight of the barrier, because the underbrush grew thick and dense off to their left. Jarvey felt bewildered, on the verge of panic. Moving from the theater of Junius Midion to the ship and then the town had been disorienting enough, but this wandering in the wilderness threw his sense of direction completely off. They had to pick their way through the trees and brush, and now and again some animal bellowed or howled in the distance. The air felt as thick and wet as steam. Moisture dripped from the leaves, like a slow rain, and when a drop splashed Jarvey's neck or face, it felt almost as warm as blood.

As they pushed on, the trees on either side of them crowded thicker and darker, and the trailing vines looped down as if trying to slow their progress. Finally they hit a thicket they couldn't force their way through, a tangled barrier of thorny vines and interwoven saplings. "No good," Betsy panted. "We'd need saws and axes to cut our way through this mess."

"Go back?" Jarvey asked.

"Can you find the way?"

Jarvey shook his head. "I got lost about five minutes after they threw us out," he confessed. He squirmed. He didn't like the heavy, humid gloom under the trees, or the sense that the screeching, yowling animal sounds had been coming closer. They climbed over the tortuous roots of a huge tree with a lumpy, knotted trunk, its dark gray bark deeply grooved in an odd diamond pattern. "Let's rest," Jarvey said.

They sat on one of the gnarled roots, and Betsy leaned back, squinting up into the green canopy overhead. "If we could only see the sky, we might have some sense of direction. We could at least judge the time."

"But we can't," Jarvey said. "Maybe—"

The root beneath him moved, surging slowly. Jarvey yelped in surprise and leaped up, and Betsy scrambled to her feet at the same time.

The tree opened two huge misshapen eyes and stared at them.

Jarvey felt frozen. Two round lumps on the trunk of the tree had split, and the splits had widened. Vast eyes, pale woody brown with black pupils, gazed at him without any trace of emotion. Beneath the eyes a horizontal slash opened—a mouth of sorts—and in a weirdly creaking voice, the tree spoke: "The hunt has begun. The Nawab has entered the forest."

"Hunt?" Betsy said, her voice rising in pitch. "What's being hunted?"

"You are," the tree said. The eyes and mouth closed and sealed themselves. A moment later it was just a tree again.

"Oh, no," Betsy said.

"He's hunting for us," Jarvey said. "He's somewhere in the jungle."

"Worse than that, he's hunting us. We could wind up with our heads hanging on his trophy wall or something! Come on. We can't stay here."

They trudged on, winding between stands of trees, pausing every so often to listen for sounds of pursuit. Hours dragged by, a long, dreary time of trying to find a passageway through the forest, backtracking, and trying again—long, exhausting, frustrating work. They heard nothing but the clamor of birds and the buzz and rattle of insects. "This is hopeless," Jarvey gasped. "We don't know which way we're going. We don't know where the Nawab is. We don't even—"

A clatter of wings and an explosion of high-pitched shrieks burst out not far away. Jarvey spun around and saw a dozen or more bright green birds speeding through the trees, dodging the trunks and banking to the left and right as they fled some disturbance. One of the birds wheeled sharply in the air and landed on a branch just above Betsy's head, ruffling its feathers and shaking its wings. It was the color of a parrot, but it didn't look like any parrot Jarvey had ever seen, but more like a smaller version of a vulture, despite its coloring.

From its perch above them, the bird cocked a beady eye at Betsy and opened its beak. "Here they are! Here they are!"

Jarvey picked up a chunk of wood and threw it at the bird. He missed, but it squawked and flew away in the direction taken by the others in its flock. "Some hunt," Jarvey said. "Everything in the forest is aware! If the Nawab gets tired of hunting us, he just has to ask a tree, or a bird, or a dumb lizard! Maybe even the rocks!"

"I wonder if the trees move," Betsy said. "Because if they do—"

"Ugh! Don't even talk about it!"

"No," Betsy said urgently. "If the trees can move, don't you see, they're *herding* us. We have to fight against them. I had the strangest feeling back there in the thicket that the trees somehow got closer together as we neared them. I think they were deliberately shutting us off. If we could get past them, we might get away. Or at least we might find the wall."

"Okay," Jarvey said. "I guess it's worth a try."

"This way."

They broke off in a new direction, and sure enough, the trees began to grow closer and closer together. They came to another thicket, or maybe just an extension of the first one, close-packed and impenetrable. "What now?" Jarvey asked.

"We go over it," Betsy said grimly. "That one there is tall enough. Climb quick, take it by surprise."

She led the way to a tree that had bent, crooked branches sprouting from the trunk almost from the ground up. She scaled up into the tree, climbing from branch to branch almost the way she would have climbed a ladder, and Jarvey followed her, scrambling as fast as he could. The branches began to tremble under his hands, and then something grabbed his foot.

At first, Jarvey thought he had snagged his foot in the fork of a twig. He jerked his leg, and whatever had his ankle only tightened. He looked down in irritation and thought he would faint. A snake had seized his ankle, a thin green snake!

He almost lost his hold on the branch and actually slipped down a few inches. The green coil on his ankle loosened— it wasn't a snake after all, he saw, just one of those hanging vines. He reached down to tear it loose, and it whipped forward, wrapping itself around his wrist. "Aghh!"

"What's wrong?" Betsy was already high above him. The thinner branch she had seized was swaying ominously, as if trying to throw her off. She looked down, then descended toward him. "Here, I'll help."

Another loop of the vine seized her wrist, and when she jerked back, it tightened. "What is this thing?"

"It's some kind of trap." Jarvey took a few deep breaths. "Don't fight it, Bets. It's worse if you pull against it." He had gone limp, and he cautiously pulled his ankle out of the loosening loop. "I don't think it wants to hurt us. It's just trying to keep us from climbing."

Betsy had grabbed the vine and tugged at it, trying to rip it in two. She winced as a loop of the rope-like thing flipped toward her head, as if trying to choke her.

"Don't fight it!" Jarvey said urgently. "Look, I'm loose."

With a shudder, Betsy relaxed her arm, and the loop of green vine unwound until she was able to slip her wrist out. "All right. It wants us to come down. I see. Ready?"

"For what?"

"Climb!" Betsy clambered up the branches, nearly leaping in her haste, reaching for one, grabbing it, hauling herself up, and already grabbing the next.

Jarvey swung himself up after her, dreading the clutch of another vine. He heard the twigs beneath him swish as the vine lashed toward him, even felt the slap of the vine against his foot, but it just missed. "Come on!" urged Betsy from far overhead. "I can see—"

She screamed as the tree *threw* her. That was the only

word for it. The branch that she was on whipped up and down, like a person shaking water off one hand, and Betsy lost her hold. Jarvey made a desperate grab, closed his hand on her wrist, and felt himself nearly jerked out of the tree himself. The vine caught up with them and wrapped itself around their ankles, tugging them toward the earth.

"It's no good," Jarvey said. "It won't let us."

"All right," Betsy said. "All right, you—you plant! We're climbing down!"

"What did you see?" Jarvey asked.

"The wall," Betsy said. "I'll tell you when we're down."

The vine refused to release its hold on them until they reached the ground. As they touched the earth again, it unlooped, freeing them. "The trees are even thicker now than they were when we started to climb," Jarvey said. "They do move somehow."

"Magic," Betsy said. "The wall's over that way. Not too far. I could see the roofs of the buildings in the town. Harbor's off to the right. I could just glimpse some of the masts. Maybe if we—"

A monkey leaped into the tree overhead, stared down at them, and started to shriek. "We can't stay here," Jarvey said. "Let's go."

They tried to head in the direction of the wall, but the

going was treacherous, broken ground cut by the twisting roots of ancient trees. "Maybe you could try some magic of your own," Betsy said.

"How?" Jarvey was tired, his hands were blistered, and he felt slimy with his own sweat. "I command the trees not to move! I order the vines not to grab us! Stay away, monkeys! I'll blast you with my power! Think that will work?"

"You don't have to be nasty. If you can't help, you can't."

"It's not my fault!" Jarvey yelled.

And at that instant the world exploded.

For a heartbeat, Jarvey thought he had been shot. White light filled the world, a sound like a cannon going off next to his head shook him to his bones, a burst of heat and a stench of burning filled the air . . .

Betsy was shaking him, her mouth moving, but no sound came out. No. Jarvey blinked and heard only the ringing of his own ears. The sound had been so loud that it had deafened him. "What?"

Betsy didn't reply in words, but yanked him to his feet— he had gone sprawling to the ground—and dragged him forward. He saw a gap in the thicket, a ragged, smoking hole four or five feet across. The steaming vines twitched aside as Betsy dragged him toward the opening. Thinly, as if she were standing a long way off, her voice broke through: "We can make it! Hurry!"

The trees and brush writhed, trying to send twigs and branches into the smoldering gap. Red sparks of fire crept through the dry edges of the hole, and Jarvey flinched away as they passed close to a burning branch. "Wait, I can't keep up!"

"There's the wall!"

This time he heard her better. "What did I do?"

"Made lightning strike the thicket! Or anyway, lightning did strike it!"

The trees on this side had thinned out, and the blue sky stretched overhead. "But there aren't any clouds."

"Magic," Betsy said shortly. "Come on! There's the seashore, and if we can get to that, we can get to the docks!"

Jarvey looked behind them. The blasted thicket was already closing up, though a thin haze of blue-gray smoke still drifted from it. From this side, the barrier looked as if it ran for miles away from the wall, following the rise and roll of the hills. Somewhere back in there the Nawab was hunting. No wonder the poster had warned about his intent.

He hunted people.

They had come to the edge of a steep drop. The cliff led almost vertically down ten or twelve feet to a row of dunes. "We can climb it," Betsy said, studying the vegetation spilling over the top of the crag. "We can hold on to these vines."

"No, thanks. They might hold on to us."

Betsy prodded one with her toe. It swayed back and forth but did not react. "Don't think so. These seem ordinary. I think the stuff in the forest might be enchanted to have some strange kind of movement, but these are just plants."

"Okay," Jarvey said. "Let's try."

It wasn't a pleasant climb, especially with his raw, blistered hands, but Jarvey followed Betsy down to the crest of a dune of coarse gray sand. The ocean rolled in a few yards away, low waves breaking and boiling on the beach. The sun had sunk toward the horizon off to the left, and it looked swollen and red. "We don't have much time until night," Jarvey said. "We were in there all day."

"We do better in the dark, anyway," Betsy pointed out. "Come on."

They made their way toward the docks, perhaps half a mile distant. Jarvey could see the masts of three or four ships, and out at sea another vessel stood away from the shore, tilting to the left as the wind filled its sails and took it out to sea. Soon they were walking through a scatter of driftwood, broken masts, snarls of fishing nets, even a snapped-off oar or two. An upended ship's boat, its bottom staved in, stuck up out of the sand like a beached whale, its surface roughened by knots of barnacles.

At last they scaled a low stone wall and stood at the end of the docks. The pier where their ship had tied up was about halfway down. By then the sun had set, and a deep twilight had fallen.

"Let's get to the hideout and retrieve the Grimoire," Betsy said. "Then we'll hide on a ship until morning."

"Okay," Jarvey said. He wondered if the Nawab was still hunting them. Maybe his spies had told him of their escape. Maybe he was coming this way right now to find them.

In the rising darkness, they darted from doorway to doorway, down alleys and over fences, until they reached the warehouse. "Hope those snakes are gone," Jarvey said. "I'll check it out."

He told himself that the cobras had only been guards. They hadn't wanted to bite him, just to drive him and Betsy out into the forest, that was all.

But now—well, if the snakes knew that they had escaped from the Nawab, what then?

To his relief, the alley stretched dark and empty. With Betsy close behind him, he felt his way down the fence until he located the loose board and pulled it to one side. Betsy slipped in before he could tell her to wait, and he followed.

It was gloomy inside the hut, but Jarvey felt absurdly relieved. They were home, as far as they could be said to have a home in this world.

"Get the Grimoire," Betsy said, dragging the crate over.

Jarvey climbed up on it, teetered, and felt around on top of the beam. "Oh, no."

"What is it?"

Jarvey didn't answer for a moment. He could feel the layer of dust on the beam, could even feel the rough patch where the Grimoire had rubbed the dust off. But as for the book itself . . .

"It's gone," he said. "Someone's taken it."

I I

Brotherhood of Evil

*T*he boat rocked. In the distance the lights of Port
Midion gleamed against the face of night. "I don't
like this," Jarvey said.

"I'm not fond of it myself," Betsy returned. "But I'd
rather be here than somewhere those cobra things could
reach us."

Jarvey had to agree with that. They had taken a fishing
boat, about a dozen feet long, and had rowed out into the
bay, where they dropped the boat's small anchor. Now
they bobbed about a mile off shore, trusting to the night
to hide them. The waves weren't large, but they occasion-

134

ally slapped the boat with a slushing sound and a salty spray of water.

"The one hunting us must be the Nawab," Jarvey said miserably. "He was the one who sent the cobras, the one who hunted us. And if he's a Midion, he'll know all about the Grimoire."

"We'll have to get it back."

"How?"

"You're the magician," Betsy pointed out.

"You keep saying that!" Jarvey fought to keep his anger down. "Look, Betsy, I don't know how to work magic. When I try, weird things happen. I make lightning strike! I can't control it. I could kill us both."

"Or not. You have the art, Jarvey. You may not be able to control it, but you have it, and I don't. If you could learn—"

"Yeah, right, if I could learn, I'd be great," Jarvey said bitterly. "I could make my own world, just like old Junius. Have an army of ghosts to serve me. Or I could turn the tables on the Nawab, couldn't I? Make the cobras and the trees and the birds obey me, not him."

"What's wrong with that?"

Jarvey grunted. "I don't know. Maybe nothing. Maybe if someone used the Grimoire for good and not for evil, it would change it somehow."

"Except I don't think anyone who's used it has thought of himself as evil," Betsy said slowly.

"Oh, come on. Tantalus Midion kidnapped about a thousand people from Earth and made them his servants. Junius has trapped his family for all eternity, and his kids can't even grow up and get away from him. This Nawab guy hunts people!"

"But Tantalus created Lunnon so he'd have a place to feel safe and a place to have power," Betsy pointed out. "He thought he'd make a city that ran properly, don't you see? And Junius really believed he was a great actor and a great playwright. The way he saw it, he was just making himself a place where his genius would be recognized."

"You're saying they aren't evil?" Jarvey asked sarcastically. "What about Siyamon? He locked my parents up in his book, and he tried to do the same thing to me! Don't tell me that's not evil!"

"It is to you," Betsy said. "But what about to him? Maybe your father was due to inherit the Grimoire, and Siyamon thought it should be his and his alone. From his point of view, he'd waited all his life to own and use the Grimoire, and here's this stranger, this foreigner, coming in and—"

"My dad didn't want the stupid old book!" Jarvey

snapped. "And if he had inherited it, he sure wouldn't do anything with it that would hurt anybody. Don't tell me that Siyamon's not evil."

"What would you do with the Grimoire, if you mastered it?" Betsy asked.

Jarvey didn't answer for a minute. Then he said, "Use it to free everyone it's got locked away. Get rid of the worlds the Midion sorcerers have created."

"So everyone in my world would die," Betsy said.

"No—"

"Yes. If you made Lunnon cease to exist, then all my friends, everyone you knew there, they would die. We can't go to your world, Jarvey. There's no room for us there. So to us, you'd be evil, do you see? You might not mean to be, but you would be."

"There's no use talking about it," Jarvey said glumly. "We've lost it."

"No, we're going to get it back somehow," Betsy corrected him. "And then we'll decide how best you can use it." She shifted herself on the seat. "You try to get some sleep. I'll take first watch. I'll wake you when I think about four hours have passed."

Jarvey couldn't lie down in the boat, because it was rolling and pitching too much, and besides, about an inch of water had collected in the lowest part. He halfway lay down on one of the hard, uncomfortable seats, gripped the gunwale, the side of the boat, with his left hand, and tried to relax, thinking about the Grimoire and what it could do.

In the beginning, he had thought that his parents, that he himself, that the whole city of Lunnon were actually in the book, were part of its pages. But Zoroaster had said the book didn't hold worlds, but opened a gateway to them. It somehow warped reality, made a hole in time and in space, and let people from one world slip through it into another. He was beginning to think that this world, that the theater of Junius Midion, that Lunnon, all existed in places that had their own reality. The dimensions, the realities, whatever you called them, existed before the Midions tampered with them. But the Midions wrote chapters in the book that were actually magic spells, and these complex spells changed the dimensions to the liking of the magicians. Maybe the cobras here weren't Earthly cobras at all, but some kind of native animal changed and reshaped by the spell that let the Nawab come through from Earth. Even the sentient trees might be plants native to the world that the magician had changed.

Or had used the Grimoire to change. Just before he

drifted to sleep, Jarvey had a final, disturbing thought. Maybe he could use the Grimoire to warp the world, all right.

But when he did, if he did . . .

Maybe the Grimoire could warp *him* at the same time.

The eastern sky was barely pink with dawn when they rowed back to shore and tied the boat up to the same pier from which they had borrowed it. No one was awake yet.

"Okay," Jarvey said. "I'm going to try a spell. I did it once before in Lunnon, when a policeman was after me. Zoroaster said it wasn't really an invisibility spell. It just made people overlook me, not notice me. I did it once, so I should be able to do it again."

"All right. Try it."

Jarvey closed his eyes and began to chant: "No one will see me. Everyone will ignore me. No one will know I am there." He said it over and over, clenching his hands.

"Nothing's happening."

"I'm trying!" He balled his fists even tighter and chanted again, faster, more urgently.

"Jarvey, it's almost daytime. We'd better hide—"

Jarvey felt a flash of anger. "I can do it!" He repeated his chant and felt a strange, electric quiver. He opened his eyes. Everything looked dim. Betsy stood looking anxiously around her.

"How's that?" Jarvey asked.

Betsy didn't reply. She looked around, her gaze sweeping right past him.

I did it, Jarvey thought. She can't see me! He nudged her, and she took a few uncertain steps away. She turned and looked around again, her face clenched in a puzzled frown. She looked as if she were on the verge of speaking, but then shook her head and walked away. Jarvey followed her.

He watched her snitch some bread for her breakfast, expertly. Jarvey simply walked into the shop and picked up a piece of the bread, eating it as the cooks chattered around him, talking of the ship that had come in with dyed fabric and cheap jewelry. No one paid him the least bit of attention. They stepped around him, never bumped into him, but they didn't seem to see him at all. Now all he had to do was . . .

"Let me go! I've done nothing!"

Betsy's voice, coming from outside the booth! Jarvey ducked out, and what he saw made his heart sink. One of those gorillas had grabbed Betsy's wrist and was dragging her along the cobbled street. She was stumbling after her captor, trying not to fall.

Jarvey hurried after her. "I'm here!" he whispered.

She still didn't seem to hear him. She was flailing at the gorilla's huge hand, crying and pleading.

The ape's nostrils twitched. Its brown eyes narrowed in suspicion, and it looked right at Jarvey. Maybe the spell didn't work with animals! Jarvey began to back away.

But the gorilla sniffed again, then tugged Betsy along. Jarvey breathed a little easier, and he fell into step behind the two. He suspected they were going his way.

And sure enough, the ape hauled Betsy along to the park, through the gate, between the guardian cobras. Jarvey had a nasty moment when he passed between them, but the snakes paid him no attention. Only when they had passed through the park did he finally see the palace, a shining white building with a multitude of towers, turrets, and domes, something like the pictures of the Taj Mahal he had seen.

The ape held tight to a struggling Betsy with one hand while it raised a heavy bronze knocker with the other. The knocker sounded like thunder in the distance, hollow, echoing booms. A moment later, the door opened and a man stood staring down at Betsy. "So here's the one causing the trouble," the man said. "I will take her to the master."

The gorilla released its hold on Betsy as the man seized her other arm. She tried to pull away, and the man, with an irritated snarl, said, "Stop that, you fool! The serpents know you're here. You won't get far, even if you pull away."

Jarvey took advantage of that moment to slip past them. No one, not the man, the gorilla, not even Betsy, noticed him. The man dragged Betsy inside and closed the door. "Come with me."

As quietly as he could, Jarvey followed in their wake, down a carpeted hall. They stepped out into an airy room, its walls crimson and hung with trophy heads. Jarvey saw the head of a great cat, something like a lion, and other heads that sprouted weirdly shaped horns. He didn't look too closely at the top row. They looked too . . . human.

Two men stood across the room, bending over a table. "My lord," the servant said, "the guard has just brought this."

One of the men, young, athletic-looking, and blond, turned around. "Ah, my quarry," he said. "Well, you must be the clever one, damaging my property the way you did. Is this the person who caused you so much trouble, brother?"

The other man turned around then, and it was all Jarvey could do not to yell out in surprise and alarm.

"No," said the displeased, dry voice of Junius Midion.

Jarvey sat huddled in a corner, hoping that his magic spell wouldn't wear off. He had watched as the blond man ordered Betsy locked up in an adjoining room, and now he listened as the two brothers argued heatedly. "Kill her, Haimish," Junius said. "And then find the other one, the boy. He's the one who took this." He rested a hand on the Grimoire, which lay atop the table.

Haimish Midion, the blond man, lifted his cane and gently nudged Junius's hand away from the book. "My dear brother, you always want to act so rashly. Kill her? Why kill her when we can use her as bait? If we let the town know that I'm holding her as a prisoner here, I'll wager the rogue will hear of it and will come to save her. People are so predictable, you see, just as in those dreary dramas of yours."

"Do whatever you want, but do it quickly and let me go back," Junius growled. "You know how the theater begins to decay if attention is not paid."

"It's not my fault you created such a shoddy little spell," Haimish retorted. "My world could function quite well without me. I've built up a whole civilization: Port Midion, and six other cities that provide us with our little luxuries. Of course, my people are real, not ghostly automatons."

"Don't tell me how to run my life," Junius said. Looking at the two of them side by side, Jarvey could tell they were brothers. Both of them had the dark, glittering blue eyes of the Midion family, and both of them had streaks of reddish hair interwoven with the blond. Junius looked at his brother with evident distaste. "And you will not disparage my art, Haimish. If I had not thought quickly and diverted him into your world, the boy might have gone anywhere. Without my warning, you would not even have known of this . . ." Junius reached to caress the book's cover.

Again, Haimish moved his cane to sweep Junius's fingers aside. "No, kindly leave the Grimoire alone, Junius."

"I shall take it back with me, of course," Junius Midion said carelessly as he stepped back from the table.

"You shall do no such thing. Oh, you managed to warn me to look for the Grimoire, but I remind you, my servants found it. It is mine. Remember, I shall use it to send you back, of course, but after doing so, I shall see that it is safely kept."

"Safely kept?" sneered Junius. "You just admitted the

people in this world of yours are real. It would be far safer with me, where there are only the actor automatons and the spectral audience. No one in my world could use the book."

"How about that son of yours, that frustrated young Augustus?" countered Haimish. "Oh, dear, I can just imagine what might happen should he get his hands on the Grimoire. You know what would occur should he open the book to your chapter whilst in your world, of course."

"The spell would reverse," Junius said. "It would cast our whole family back into our time and place on Earth, and we would age and die. Of course I'd let them all know that, and that would be enough—"

"No, it would not be enough," Haimish said smoothly. "Not nearly enough, not when your theater-mad family is involved. If you go back to Earth, the book goes back to Earth as well, and I'll not have the gateway to my world available to any meddling fool who can use a simple spell."

Junius glared at his brother with something like hatred. "Need I remind you that I am the elder?"

"And I am the wiser. Junius, be reasonable. I agreed to consult with you and learn why this book has turned up here, of all places. It poses us quite a problem, but after all, I have the Grimoire, Junius, and here it shall remain." Haimish Midion picked up the book, crossed the room, and stopped in front of a massive desk. He fished in his pocket for a key, unlocked a drawer of the desk, and dropped the book inside. "There it shall rest until we find this boy, and once we have dealt with him, I shall use it to send you back to your poor decaying theater. But I shall keep it, make no mistake."

Junius had been watching him with an expression of rage. "Oh, very well! We shall decide what to do with the Grimoire in due time. But first capture that wretched boy, Haimish."

"If only you could tell me his full name. A good magician can control anything if he knows its true name, but of course you have no idea, do you?" Haimish asked in a nasty tone.

"I may not know his full name, but I warn you, he is a Midion. He said he was, and anyway, I could recognize him by his features—eyes midnight blue, hair like rusty gold, all that. He may be dangerous."

"How old is he?"

Junius shrugged. "I don't know. Twelve, thirteen perhaps."

"Then his training surely is nowhere near complete. I

can deal with any trifling spells he might have mastered."

"You couldn't find him in your precious forest!"

Haimish shrugged. "Peasants are so easy to hunt. I fear my abilities as a stalker have become dulled by hunting mere criminals. Yes, I agree, I should have had the two wretches brought here to the palace. I thought it would be fun to hunt some real game for a change, and that was a mistake. He used a lightning spell! Crude, crude, but so crude I did not expect it."

"What if he does it again? What if he blasts your animal guards?" Junius sounded upset and angry. "If he got close enough, he might even destroy the Grimoire with a spell like that, and you know that would be the end of us!"

Haimish snorted. "He won't even be able to try, not in town. My magic rules here, you know. Come, it is time to eat. I shall send my servants to post notices in town. Anyone who finds him and brings him here will be exempt from the hunt forever, him and all his family. That will make people eager to find our young Midion for us. Do you know, I almost hope this boy has some real power. I haven't had a really challenging hunt in so long now. . . ." Still talking, Haimish escorted Junius from the room.

Jarvey immediately hurried over to the desk. It was enormous, made of some heavy, very dark wood. He tugged at the drawer, found it firmly locked, as he had expected, and hunted around for something to use to break the lock. Nothing. He heard the door rattling, and realized that in the next room Betsy was trying to find a way out.

He paused, biting his lip. If he opened the door, Betsy would ignore him, because of the spell he had cast. If she slipped away, the cobras might get her, or Haimish might hunt her. She was safer locked up, at least for the moment.

Jarvey found a poker in a stand in front of the fireplace, but it was too big and clumsy to use. A pair of crossed swords over the mantel offered a possibility. He dragged a chair over, climbed on it, and took down one of the swords, but its blade was too thick to force into the crack around the desk drawer. Jarvey was feeling more and more frustrated and upset. All he needed was something to open the stupid drawer. He made a fist and pounded on it once.

Crack! The wood split with a sound almost as loud as a pistol shot, making Jarvey jump in surprise. He opened his hand and looked at it in wonder. Had he just worked another spell? He must have. The wood was thick and tough, and yet a half-inch wide crack had opened right across the top of the drawer. He tugged at the handle, and the drawer creaked out of the desk, just far enough to let him reach in and pull out the Grimoire.

Then he crossed to the locked door, turned the latch, and the door swung open. Betsy had hauled chairs over and was climbing up, trying to get over the transom. She looked down in shock. "Jarvey!"

She could see him again. "Come on. I've got the book. We have to—"

"Stop right there!"

Jarvey spun around. Haimish and Junius Midion had burst into the room, and they stood staring furiously at him. Haimish had raised his cane and waved it, reciting some spell.

"Grab my arm!" Jarvey yelled, opening the catch of the Grimoire. Betsy grabbed the book instead, but he had no time to lose.

Just as Junius and Haimish Midion shouted out spells of their own, Jarvey yelled, *"Abrire ultimas!"*

The Grimoire writhed, and with explosions of light all around him, Jarvey plunged into the unknown.

12

Comforts of Home

It was like being on a runaway amusement-park ride, and the spinning made him feel deathly sick. He and Betsy were holding on to the Grimoire, but they were on opposite sides, and they were whirling around each other, so it was hard to hold on. Jarvey felt his grip begin to slip on the leather cover, and desperately he tightened his fingers.

No use! He lost his hold, clawed frantically at nothing but air, and then he felt himself flipping head over heels and heels over head through a dark, terrible tunnel. He couldn't yell, he couldn't see, he couldn't even breathe. It felt as though he were free-falling from a great height, and he cringed as he imagined the bone-shattering impact.

But it never came. Jarvey opened his eyes in darkness. He lay tangled in sheets, and he was sweating so much he felt soaked. Jarvey kicked and writhed and flailed until he had unwrapped himself, flipped over onto his stomach, and then he saw the red digital display of his clock radio: 5:10.

"No," he groaned. It was all happening again. He felt around until he located the lamp on his bedside table and switched it on. Warm light flooded his room, and this time it *was* his room, without any doubt, red curtains, black blinds, his junk on the desk, his clothes on the floor, everything in place, just as he remembered it from dreams, from real life.

The air felt hot, though, very hot, and stuffy. He went to the raised window and leaned his head against the screen, feeling the cool touch of morning air on his forehead and cheeks. He could see his yard outside, dimly illuminated by the one light far down at the end of the cul-de-sac. Crickets chirped and chattered in the flower beds. Jarvey took a deep breath and then padded barefoot out to his parents' bedroom door. He hesitated for only a moment before rapping on it with his knuckles, quickly but softly, *rat-tat-tat.*

He heard his dad's sleepy voice: "Hmm? What is it? Come in."

Jarvey pushed the door open. "Dad? Mom?"

His father clicked his bedside lamp on and sat up, his hair sticking every which way as he fumbled around on his bedside table for his glasses. "Jarvey? What time is it? What's wrong? House on fire?"

Jarvey stood in the doorway, breathing hard. The rumpled man sitting up in the bed was his father, Dr. Cadmus Midion, and the sleepy-looking woman just getting up on her elbows was his mother, Samantha. "Are you guys okay?" Jarvey asked in a small voice.

"What's wrong, sweetheart?" his mom asked, brushing her hair back out of her eyes. She sounded startled and concerned.

His dad had finally found his glasses, and he peered through them at his watch. "Five fifteen on a Saturday morning! This is a fine way to start your summer vacation, son. What's wrong?"

"I—I thought I heard something," Jarvey stammered. "A kind of—of explosion sound."

"Thunder?" his mother asked, reaching for her robe. "Is it raining?"

"No," Jarvey said. "It—it wasn't really like thunder. Just a kind of boom."

His father yawned. "Um. Sonic boom, maybe. Jet flying over very fast, but I didn't hear anything. Did you, Samantha?"

"No." Jarvey's mom put her cool hand on his forehead. "Are you sure it wasn't a dream, sweetheart?"

Jarvey didn't think he had a fever, though his face felt hot with embarrassment. "Um, I don't know, Mom. What day is today?"

"It's Saturday," his mother said promptly. "Oh, the date? It's the first day of summer break."

"For you, anyway," his dad added. "I still have finals left to give before college is out for a week. Come on, what did you think you heard, Jarvey?"

Jarvey shook his head. "Must've been a dream, I guess. It's all mixed up." He paused and then said, "Dad, what's a grimoire?"

His father's eyebrows rose in evident surprise. "A what?"

"A grimoire," Jarvey said. "It's a word I, uh, heard somewhere."

His father scratched his head, further ruffling his brownish-blond hair. "Book of some kind, isn't it? Like a book about magic and that sort of thing?"

"Do we have one?"

Samantha Midion guided Jarvey over and made him sit on the foot of the bed. "Jarvey, you're not making a lot of sense. What are you talking about?"

"I thought there was a Midion Grimoire," Jarvey said slowly. "A book of magical spells and stuff. Over in England."

His mother and father exchanged a questioning glance. Then his dad said, "That must have been one doozy of a dream. Well, I've never heard of a Midion Grimoire, in England or anywhere else. I seem to associate grimoires with medieval alchemists, the guys who kept trying to turn lead into gold, without much success. Anyway, it's an odd time of the morning to get curious about old books. Right now I'd suggest that you go back to bed and back to sleep for at least two more hours, champ. This is summer break! Get the most out of it!"

"Okay." Jarvey pulled away from his mother's arm and plodded out. He felt strangely dizzy and disoriented. The whole house was hot. Back in his room he switched on the radio and moved the pointer up and down the dial until he found a public radio station that was broadcasting the news. According to the newscaster, the temperature was in the high seventies and the date was the third of June. But wait, they had flown to England on the afternoon of June 6, hadn't they?

Or had it been a dream?

Jarvey pinched himself, and the pinch hurt. He'd read or heard somewhere that you could wake yourself from a bad dream if you could pinch yourself hard enough, but nothing happened. What did that prove? He couldn't get back to sleep, and so he dressed quietly and tiptoed downstairs. He opened the door and looked out across the quiet lawn. Vaguely he remembered something terrible about the moon, but he couldn't see a moon at all, just the scattered, fading stars of early morning. He went back inside, to the family room, and switched on the TV.

Old movies, infomercials selling everything from get-rich-quick books to machines designed to make you lose weight, reruns of old, old TV shows, news and weather, everything looked normal as he used the remote to surf the channels. And the on-screen display agreed that today was the third of June, and if the year was right, he was still eleven until Thursday rolled around.

But how could that be? Jarvey remembered months and months of other things happening. He remembered . . . what was her name? A red-haired girl who had helped him somehow. And Lunnon, a place called Lunnon, and a theater. No, he thought with a frown, the theater had to be part of a dream, a building as big as the whole world, ghosts in the seats, a strange family acting out the plays. Couldn't be real. For that matter, time got all messed up in dreams. Sometimes he'd had nightmares of playing baseball, of smacking a good, sharp line drive and then running toward first base, except he was running in slow motion, hardly able to drag one foot in front of the other, while the other players raced around the field to scoop up the ball, make the throw to first, and put him out.

Still . . . still, he remembered, vaguely, a whole series of things that had to take weeks, if not months.

Restless, he switched off the TV and went back up to his room. His wall calendar had June 9 circled in red and in the space next to the date, in his own handwriting, were the words "Baseball tryouts." He wanted to . . . to pitch, that was it. This year he wanted to pitch. He'd been practicing. Donny Russell was good, but Jarvey thought he could beat him at pitching, could . . . could get the position. . . .

But hadn't tryouts already happened? He tried to remember and thought of the big chain-link fence around the field and . . . a big spider? No. This must have been a dream, he told himself.

But he had to miss the tryouts, because they were set for the Friday after his family had flown to Lunnon. No, to . . . to London. To Hag's Court, the place was called.

He went back down to the den and turned on the computer. There was one way to check. He started the Internet browser his dad used and did a search for "Hag's Court in London." The search engine responded "Your search did not produce any result." Okay, then, he thought, how about grimoire? This time he found an article that told him a grimoire was a book of magical information written between medieval times and the eighteenth century. The word came from Old French and was akin to grammar, because a grimoire dealt with the structures of magic spells, as a grammar book dealt with the structure of sentences . . . and so on. Nothing about the Midion Grimoire anywhere. Nothing about the Midions, for that matter, at least his own family.

His mom and dad came downstairs at about eight, dressed but still looking a little sleepy. "You feeling better, champ?" his dad asked at the breakfast table.

"Yeah," Jarvey said slowly. "I guess I am. I had a really weird dream last night. I thought we flew to England because you came into an inheritance."

Dr. Cadmus Midion laughed. "I wish! I'm afraid we're

pretty much stuck at home this summer, because I've agreed to teach three summer session classes at the college. But we've been talking about a vacation. Maybe next year we'll actually be able to go to London, Paris, and Rome for a couple of weeks. We'll see."

They ate their cornflakes, and when his dad finished reading the morning paper, Jarvey took it to his room and went through it page by page. It was the ordinary, everyday local paper, with a big front-page story about the building of a new church, another about a car crash that destroyed a truck and a car but didn't hurt anyone too badly, and other stories about normal commonplace things. Even the comic strips were familiar.

His dad began mowing the lawn, the same exact way he had mowed it the week before they drove to the airport to fly to London—no, that hadn't happened. But as he started out to help, Jarvey paused to pour his dad a tall glass of ice water and thought, I've done this before. He tried to shrug off the feeling and took the glass out to his dad. "Thanks, son," Dr. Midion said, taking a long sip and then fishing out his handkerchief to wipe his sweaty face.

Jarvey shivered, and thought to himself, He's going to say this will be a scorcher of a summer and he wonders if it's because of global warming.

"Hot already," his dad remarked. "Going to be a scorcher of a summer, I think. I wonder if global warming is causing this."

Jarvey closed his eyes. He had been here and done this already. He felt that he already knew everything his dad was going to say and do. The letter would come by noon, the long creamy envelope all the way from London, England, instructing Dr. Midion to be present on June 8 for the reading of the will of Thaddeus Midion, late of Hag's Court.

But he forced a smile and took over the lawn mower, trimming the front lawn into increasingly smaller rectangles until he finished the job. His mom made lemonade for the family, and sitting at the table and sipping from the tall, frosty glass, Jarvey asked, "What is it when you already know what's going to happen? When it's like you've lived through that moment before?"

His mother frowned a little. "You mean déjà vu? That's sort of a psychological state, I think."

"French term," his father put in. "It means 'already seen.' It's kind of a creepy sense that everything that is happening right now has happened before. I read somewhere that it's caused by a lag between what you see or hear and the way your brain processes the information."

Slowly, Jarvey said, "I think you're going to get a letter from England today, Dad."

"I don't think I've ever received a letter from England in my whole life," Dr. Midion said, sounding surprised. "What makes you say that, son?"

Jarvey shrugged, feeling helpless.

Time crawled by until noon, and when the mail carrier drove her little truck down the street, Jarvey went out to meet her. She handed him a bundle of letters, magazines, and catalogs, and he sorted through them as he walked back to the house. A magazine about history that his dad subscribed to, catalogs from clothing stores and gift stores, a water bill from the county, three or four credit-card offers from banks, and a square envelope addressed to Jarvey. Probably a birthday card, he guessed, since his birthday was coming up in a couple of days.

No heavy, creamy envelope with foreign stamps on it. Jarvey breathed a sigh of relief as he dropped the mail into the basket on the hall table. "Mail's here," he called, and then he took the square envelope addressed to him up to his room.

Sprawling down on the bed, Jarvey tore it open, and took out the card inside. Huh, he thought, strange kind of birthday card. No picture on it at all, just a blank white card, folded. Maybe it had a funny message inside.

He opened it up and found the inside of the card was just as blank and white as the outside: no picture, no funny saying, no check from his grandmother, nothing at all. He turned the card over and over, frowning at it, wondering if it was some kind of prank.

And then the card squirmed in his grasp.

Jarvey caught his breath. The white cardboard was pulsating, swelling and shrinking like a balloon. Suddenly a blister rose up on the surface, became an oval, and the oval became a white mask of a face. It opened blank eyes, and in a whispery voice, the face spoke to him: "It's not real! None of it is real!"

With a startled gasp, Jarvey flung the card away. It burst into smoke, a silent explosion, and the smoke faded.

The envelope was gone too. All evidence of the card's existence had vanished.

But Jarvey remembered the face, remembered the voice, and he recognized both of them.

"Betsy," he said.

13

This Is the Way the World Ends

Jarvey opened his eyes in darkness. He lay tangled in sheets, and he was sweating so much he felt soaked. Jarvey kicked and writhed and flailed until he had unwrapped himself, flipped over onto his stomach, and then he saw the red digital display of his clock radio: 5:10.

"No," he groaned. It was all happening again.

And then he scrambled out of bed, his heart swelling painfully in his throat. This wasn't déjà vu, and it wasn't a bad dream. He remembered the terrible spinning sensation, the fall through space, the card with Betsy's face, everything!

He wasn't home. The people in the room next to his weren't his parents. Something terrible had happened. Jarvey pulled his jeans, T-shirt, and sneakers on, then ran out to the landing, opened his parents' bedroom door, and stood breathing hard, listening.

No sound at all—he heard nothing, no breathing, no snoring, nothing. He turned on the light.

His father sat half up in bed, his hand on the bedside lamp. He was frozen in that attitude, like a department store mannequin, and beside him, Jarvey's mom was just beginning to rise from her interrupted sleep. Jarvey walked stiffly over and looked at the time on the clock. It was 5:11, a couple of minutes before he had come in.

The . . . actors weren't ready to begin yet. Staring at his father, Jarvey had the sickening sensation that something wasn't finished. Dr. Midion's skin was slick, like plastic, not like real flesh, and his hair looked strange, more like something artificial than real hair. Jarvey backed away, turned off the light, and shut the door. He stood there breathing hard for a few minutes, and then he knocked, just as he had before.

He heard his father's voice again: "Hmm? What is it? Come in."

Jarvey opened the door and said, "Who are you?"

His father clicked his bedside lamp on and sat up, his hair sticking every which way as he fumbled around on his bedside table for his glasses. "Jarvey? What time is it? What's wrong? House on fire?"

Now he looked perfect, the image of Dr. Midion. Jarvey balled his hands into fists and said, "You're not real! Who are you? What's going on?"

"What's wrong, sweetheart?" his mom asked, brushing her hair back out of her eyes. Jarvey groaned. It was his mom, it was—no, it wasn't! It was some horrible creation like the actors in Junius Midion's nightmare theater, pretending to be her.

"Is Siyamon doing this?" Jarvey demanded.

His dad had finally found his glasses, and he peered through them at his watch. "Five fifteen on a Saturday morning! This is a fine way to start your summer vacation, son. What's wrong?"

Jarvey stared at him. "You can't say anything new, can you? Siyamon somehow figured out what I would ask, and he programmed you both to answer me, just like you were real, but you can't handle anything he didn't plan for."

"Thunder?" his mother asked, reaching for her robe. "Is it raining?"

"Stop it!" Jarvey yelled. "I've been trying and trying to find you and get back to you, and he's tricked me! Stop it, I know it isn't real!"

When his mother began to step toward him, he turned and ran out of the room, down the stairs, and out onto the lawn. "Betsy!" he yelled. "Where are you? What happened?"

The earth began to shake so hard that Jarvey's teeth clicked together. He staggered and stumbled, then fell to his knees on the lawn. "No! I don't believe in this," he said fiercely. "I don't believe in Siyamon's magic and illusions! This isn't my house, and those aren't my mom and dad!"

The ground under his knees and hands felt horribly wrong, mushy and soft, like mud. He rose again and then found his feet were sinking down into the earth. Floundering, half falling, Jarvey lurched to the driveway, dragged himself up onto it, and stood there staring at what was happening to his house.

The sky had become quite light, but not with sunrise. A flat, bronze radiance lit it, and the house looked strange and unreal in that light.

And it was melting.

The house sagged horribly. A window slipped down

into a drooling hole, the roof slowly sagged downward. The whole neighborhood was becoming a plastic, soggy goo. From the hole that had been the front door a few moments earlier, his father came, taking jerky steps. "Mow the lawn," he gibbered. "Champ baseball lemonade mow lawn history college summer break baseball Jarvey lawn magic grimoire grimoire grimoire . . ."

The figure fell on its face and in a horrifying way tried to crawl forward, but like the house, it was melting and rubbery. One leg stretched thin and broke off. The fingers fell off and burrowed into the soft earth like pink worms. The eyes had fallen away behind the spectacles, and the creature stared at Jarvey with empty sockets as the dissolving mouth continued to babble in a terrible, liquid imitation of Jarvey's dad's voice: "Bebaw garrhhh jarrv ssssummmerrrrr . . . " It trailed off in a gargling bubble, and the form collapsed flat, like a balloon emptying itself of air.

Jarvey backed away, desperately hoping that his mother, or the imitation of her, would not come out. He spun around. The neighborhood had dissolved. Now before him lay an endless flat expanse of brassy, sandy earth, all the way to a distant, vague horizon. The air felt thick in his lungs, and the heat, the terrible heat, was like an oven.

When he turned back, he couldn't even find the place where the house had stood, and he saw no trace of the awful creature that had imitated his father.

But from somewhere he heard a voice, a mocking voice with an English accent: "This is the way the world ends. Not with a bang, but a whimper."

"Where are you?" Jarvey yelled. "Siyamon, where are you?"

Laughter, mocking and cold, was the only reply. "You could have them back," the voice said from everywhere at once. "Your mother, your father. Your life. All you have to do is surrender the book, you know."

The Grimore. But he had lost the Grimoire!

"No," he said, trying to sound a lot braver than he felt. "It wouldn't be real! You'd trap us in some world you created and make us believe we were home."

"Not I," the voice said, and now Jarvey began to have the feeling that it wasn't the voice of Siyamon Midion after all. It didn't sound as old, as silky, as insinuating as the old man's voice, for one thing. "My master might trouble with you, but not I. If he left matters to me, I would squash you like an insect."

Jarvey closed his eyes. Who was that? It wasn't Tantalus, or Junius, or Haimish Midion. "Where are you?" he demanded, opening his eyes again. "Let me see you!"

"I am outside," the voice responded. "And you are inside. You could let me in, though. Use the book and let me in, and then we shall talk."

Jarvey felt his anger rising. "Shut up! Liar!"

"You shall feel differently in a few hours. Or a few years. Or a few hundred years," the voice said.

Jarvey wanted to run, to pound something, to fight back. But he had nothing to fight against. He stood in the center of a flat desert beneath a featureless sky. There was nothing to hit. He felt furious at the unseen voice. "Betsy, where are you?" he yelled at the top of his lungs.

"She is lost in a book at the moment," the voice returned mockingly. "If you would simply open the book and—"

"Betsy!"

Jarvey saw something moving, and he ran toward it. He had thought it was someone lying on the sand, trying to sit up. No, what he saw was made entirely of sand. A mound of it was stirring, looking like a miniature sand dune in sped-up motion, coming toward him as he ran. He stopped a few feet away.

The sand was becoming the image of a person—of Betsy. A statue of sand, perfect in every feature, as if Betsy were crawling toward him on her stomach. The sand head looked up blindly, and the sand mouth opened. "Jarvey?" the voice asked, like Betsy's, but distant and thin.

"Here. Help me!"

"It isn't real," the sand Betsy said. "Not in the book. Not in the book. Siyamon's man, not Siyamon. Don't believe him. It isn't real. Use your art."

"I don't have any art!"

"You do. Use . . . use it. . . ."

A dry wind sprang up, and the Betsy statue dissolved, the grains of sand trailing out in long streamers. Jarvey reached for them and felt the stinging grains pelt his skin.

He knelt in the sand, his head bowed. "I don't have any art," he whispered.

But he did. He had used it in Lunnon. He had made himself unnoticeable in Haimish Midion's jungle world, had called down a bolt of lightning when he and Betsy had been trapped in the forest. How had he ?

He thought back to all the strange things that had happened around him, to the time when he had been angry because of a canceled field trip and the windows of his school had blown out. And the time when he was upset because he had made a mistake at the board, the electrical circuits in the school had fried themselves. The time when the pressure had been on him in a ball game to get a hit, and his bat had exploded as he smacked a home run.

When I'm upset, he thought. Or when I'm good and mad. That's when I can call on the art. That's when I can do magic.

And he thought of the terrible trick he had almost fallen for, of the imitation of his father and his mother. The man whose voice was taunting him had made them, had prepared the trap. He would crush Jarvey like a bug, like an insect.

Jarvey saw in memory the white, pale face of the spidery man in his nightmare. He had seen it before. When Siyamon Midion had ushered him into his car, his Rolls-Royce, that man had been at the wheel of the car. Siyamon had even mentioned his name. A strange name, not Midion, not a relative, but . . .

What was it?

Jarvey grabbed handfuls of hot sand and squeezed them. What was the name? Haimish Midion had contemptuously told his brother that a good magician could control anything if he knew its true name! And Siyamon had said the man's name. If only Jarvey could remember!

They were in the Rolls-Royce, and Siyamon was taking Jarvey to Bywater House, Siyamon's mansion outside of London. Siyamon was toying with his silver-headed cane and his voice was droning on and on. What had he said?

". . . you will enjoy a tour of my home, perhaps tomorrow, as they and I are attending the reading of the will. I shall have Mr. . . . "

Mr.—Mr. what? Siyamon had said the name, an odd name, and it was almost on the tip of Jarvey's tongue. If he knew it, he could do something. If he could remember the name, the name of—

"Henge!" Jarvey said suddenly. "Rupert Henge!"

Thunder crashed from the brassy sky. Jarvey felt a surge of anger. "Rupert Henge!" he shouted again. "This isn't real! None of this is real! I don't believe in it! *I want to see the truth! Now!*"

The world swirled around him, but Jarvey sprang to his feet and stood firm. The desert vanished as though swept away in a sandstorm. Instead of the desert, there was a room, a dim room with gray walls, and standing a few feet away from Jarvey, his expression somehow fearful and furious at once, was the pale-faced spider of a man. He raised his hands.

"Then see the truth—and die!" shouted Rupert Henge.

14

The Unwritten Future

Henge thrust his hands forward, fingers spread, and an invisible fist smashed into Jarvey, knocking him right off his feet. The wind huffed out of his lungs as he hit the wall behind him, but he didn't fall. Henge made a flapping gesture, and Jarvey slid up the wall, stuck there like a bug on a windshield. "Midions aren't the only ones who can wield the art," Henge said, a ghastly grin splitting his face.

"What—what will Siyamon say when you tell him you didn't get the book?" Jarvey gasped out.

Henge's whole face jerked in a snarl of rage. For a moment he hesitated, but then he pulled his hands back, and Jarvey plummeted five feet to the floor, landing with a shock that made him bite his tongue. He collapsed to his hands and knees and crouched there, waiting for his lungs to work properly again.

"Where is the Grimoire?" Henge asked.

"Where you'll never find it," Jarvey managed to gasp, hoping he sounded more certain than he felt.

"You thought we'd never find *you*," Henge said with a sneer. "But Master Siyamon has ways of tracking you. Especially when you sleep. Do you enjoy the dreams he sends you?"

The nightmares. Jarvey closed his eyes. Siyamon had sent the nightmares to torment him. "He thought I'd panic and use the book, didn't he?" Jarvey asked in a voice of fury. He opened his eyes and glared at Henge. "He knows when I use the book, doesn't he?"

"He is the master of the Grimoire. What do you think? Give me the book, boy."

Jarvey got unsteadily to his feet. "Where are we now?"

"That is of no importance. Give me the Grimoire."

Jarvey shook his head. "No. You can't find it, and

Siyamon wouldn't let you use it. So where are we?"

"I could make you feel greater pain than you've ever dreamed possible."

"Maybe so," Jarvey said. "But it wouldn't do you any good, not if you really want the book. Look, I'll—I'll answer a question for you if you answer one for me. Where are we? We can't be in a world created by the Grimoire."

For a long moment Henge stared at him with a look of utter hatred. "Midions," he said finally. "You are all alike, aren't you? And not just in looks. He is stubborn, too. Very well. This"—he spread his hands—"this is not a world, not as you know the ones the Grimoire leads to. It is a state of mind, a place of illusion. It can seem very real. It could be your way of being with your parents again. That's what you want, isn't it?"

Jarvey shook his head. "Not in the way you mean, not with some kind of robot *things* that talk like my parents and look like them, but that don't really exist."

"Now my question," Henge said. "Where is the book?"

"Sorry," Jarvey said softly. "You asked a question already, and I answered it."

Henge growled like an animal and drew his hand back. Jarvey, hanging on to the memory of the horrible things that had almost convinced him they were his mother and father, raised his own hands and yelled something at the same moment: "Protect me!"

Henge shot his hand forward, but a yard from Jarvey's face, the air burst into crackling flame, red, green, orange tongues curving back and around Jarvey, as though he were standing in a crystal dome and the fire couldn't reach him. He felt a numbing vibration, as if the whole world were being jackhammered apart, but he held his hands up, pushing against the magic Henge had directed at him.

The man stepped back, his chest heaving, his eyes wary. "You do have some of the art," he said. "Well, well. My master believed you would be helpless."

"Yeah, well, Siyamon's a liar. You should know that if you've worked for him long."

"I wonder, though, how long you can keep up your defense. Not long enough, I suspect." With the speed of a striking rattlesnake, Henge lashed a hand toward Jarvey.

Flinching, Jarvey tried to divert the force, but he was a second too slow. Heat washed over him, and the walls shimmered away to gray boiling mist. In an instant he stood in a featureless landscape, surrounded by ragged, roiling gray fog. Jarvey sensed rather than saw that Henge was charging him, and he quickly yelled, "Let me see!"

The fog did not dissipate, but he did see, in a way—

Henge's shape showed up as a dull red human-shaped glow, already pitching forward to grab him. Jarvey pivoted faster than he ever had on the baseball diamond, and Henge barely missed him. "You can't see me!" Jarvey said urgently, hoping with all his being that he could pull it off. "You can't see me at all!"

He backed away. Henge had rushed past him. His flickering red shape turned slowly, arms spread out. "You can't hide," he said. "Not in here. Not in my illusion."

Jarvey edged farther away, not daring to breathe loudly. He couldn't see Henge in any detail, just that vague, glowing silhouette, but from the way the figure swung its head from side to side, like a bear standing on its hind legs and swiveling to test the breeze for scents, he guessed that his spell was holding. He wasn't invisible, but Henge didn't seem to be able to locate him.

Henge let out an irritated grunt and swept his hand in a circle. The fog cleared away at once. Henge turned completely around, staring at what was again a dimly lit room. "What have you done now, boy? I know you haven't escaped. There is only one way out of this place, and I control that. Not even Siyamon could get out without my sensing it. What little mischief have you worked now?"

Jarvey didn't answer.

Henge was muttering and chanting, and Jarvey kept circling to stay behind him. He knew all too well that his own magic, his own wild art, as Siyamon had called it, was no match for someone who had studied the subject, who had been trained in it. Henge suddenly stopped. He jerked and twisted oddly, as if he were a puppet whose strings were being yanked by a madman. His angry, staring face whipped around, and Jarvey saw his features change.

Like the creatures that had pretended to be his parents, Henge was melting.

No, not melting, but reshaping. His nose grew longer, his eyes deeper, and Jarvey found himself looking at the face of old Siyamon Midion. Somehow Siyamon had invaded Henge's body and was speaking through him like a ventriloquist manipulating a dummy. "What are you doing, Henge?" his voice snapped. "Why is it taking so long?"

Henge groaned, and then answered himself, in his own voice: "Master, the boy has learned some art. He is devious."

"You have more power than any boy. Use it! Bring me the book! Quickly!"

Like a mask dissolving away, Siyamon's features faded into Henge's angry face. He seemed weak, tottering on his feet. He half staggered to one of the walls and leaned against it. "Boy! Where are you? What have you done? Show yourself and end this quickly, or it will be worse for you!"

Why hadn't Siyamon remained? Was it that he couldn't attack Jarvey himself? Or was he . . . was Siyamon afraid of him? Jarvey felt his heart thundering. Did he have more power than he thought? Was Siyamon actually frightened of facing him one-on-one?

But Siyamon had been right. Henge was some kind of magician, and if Siyamon had taught him, he had to know more magic than Jarvey did. Jarvey suddenly realized he needed help. He couldn't face Henge alone. Mentally he began to call for help, not saying anything aloud but repeating a name over and over in his mind, imagining himself shouting it: "Betsy. Betsy! Betsy!"

And something was happening. The mist was flowing back. Henge saw it too, and for the first time his ferocious expression faltered. He looked—he looked afraid.

Betsy! Betsy! I need you! Betsy!

"What are you up to?" Henge was still glaring from side to side. "You can't hide in fog, you fool. This is my illusion!" Henge barked a command, but the fog merely thickened.

Jarvey could still see Henge's form, outlined in that

flickery red light, but Henge evidently couldn't see at all. He stumbled forward, his hands stretched out, feeling his way.

Jarvey felt something, an electric sensation, like a shock. It hurt, and he yelled out without meaning to. He saw the red silhouette of Henge's head swing around toward the sound . . .

And the fog condensed, shrank in on itself, and took on shape, and a second later it had become Betsy, her face terrified.

But she held the Grimoire clutched in both arms.

Henge yelled in triumph and lunged forward. Jarvey was closer. He grabbed the book, shoved Betsy aside, and as Henge reached him, Jarvey opened the Grimoire. "You're caught!" he shouted, holding the book open but facing away from him, facing Henge.

Henge didn't even have time to cry out. Some force seized him, pulled him forward, and his body flowed into the book, fast as a bolt of lightning. Everything went dark, but Jarvey kept his grip on the book. By feel, he turned the whole block of pages. "Last chapter for us! I'm writing it!" he yelled. "Betsy! Me! Somewhere safe!"

A moment or a hundred years later, Betsy, her clothes

from Haimish Midion's world bedraggled and ragged, looked around and said, "It's very green, isn't it?"

Jarvey had just managed to hang on to the Grimoire, despite the sensation of being ripped right out of the world in which Henge had trapped him. "It's supposed to be," he said. He gave her a weak smile. "You held on to the book."

"Someone had to," she returned. "I was in that kind of billowy fog, sort of with you but not at the same time. I mean, I kept getting glimpses of you. You were in this horrid place where these awful *creatures* were wearing masks and pretending to be your parents."

Jarvey asked, "Where were you?"

Betsy shook her head. "I dunno. I think I was nearly with you. In between, sort of. I could sort of see a house, with walls and doors and all, but they were like, I dunno, like pictures painted on fog, if that makes sense. I could walk right through the walls, and you couldn't see me for the longest time. I kept trying to make you hear me."

"I finally did. You sent me a kind of birthday card. Thanks."

Betsy shrugged. "What now?"

"Now we get strong," Jarvey told her. "We can have whatever we need here. But I have to practice. I can't free my parents without fighting Siyamon. And I don't think I could win a fight with him, not yet, not even with the Grimoire. I can sort of do magic now. I have to learn to be good at it."

"Do you think you can do it? Learn magic? Control the book, and not let it trap you?"

Jarvey sighed. "I don't know, but I have to try."

Betsy bit her lip. "My grandfather," she said. "He'll help you if you can call him here."

Jarvey nodded. "Zoroaster is a good man. I'll call him here, if I can. But you'll help too, and that means a lot."

"I'll do what I can." Betsy looked around, her eyes wide with wonder. "Only—what world are we in now?"

"The very last chapter in the book. A new world. Mine."

"Oh. It's not very large, is it?"

"That's because I've just started to write it," Jarvey said. "It will get bigger. But I began with this."

They stood on a level green piece of earth, suspended in empty space. Stars shone above them—and below them too. It was as if they were traveling through the galaxy on a flat green spaceship, Jarvey thought.

Except this patch of green would grow to be as much world as they needed. It would give them room to prepare for the final battle.

"It's lovely," Betsy said. She kicked the white rubber marker. "But what is this thing? And why are we on a little hill?"

"It's the pitcher's mound," Jarvey said. "And this is what we call a baseball diamond."

THE END OF BOOK TWO